I0752632

THE MARRIAGE CONTRACT

HONORE DE BALZAC

Translated by Katharine Prescott Wormeley

The Marriage Contract

Honore de Balzac

© 1st World Library – Literary Society, 2005
PO Box 2211
Fairfield, IA 52556
www.1stworldlibrary.org
First Edition

LCCN: 2005906494

Softcover ISBN: 1-4218-1550-8
Hardcover ISBN: 1-4218-1450-1
eBook ISBN: 1-4218-1650-4

Purchase *"The Marriage Contract"*
as a traditional bound book at:
www.1stWorldLibrary.org/purchase.asp?ISBN=1-4218-1550-8

1st World Library Literary Society is a nonprofit organization dedicated to promoting literacy by:

- Creating a free internet library accessible from any computer worldwide.
- Hosting writing competitions and offering book publishing scholarships.

Readers interested in supporting literacy through sponsorship, donations or membership please contact: literacy@1stworldlibrary.org
Check us out at: www.1stworldlibrary.ORG and start downloading free ebooks today.

The Marriage Contract
contributed by Tim, Ed & Rodney
in support of
1st World Library Literary Society

DEDICATION

To Rossini

CHAPTER I

PRO AND CON

Monsieur de Manerville, the father, was a worthy Norman gentleman, well known to the Marechael de Richelieu, who married him to one of the richest heiresses of Bordeaux in the days when the old duke reigned in Guienne as governor. The Norman then sold the estate he owned in Bessin, and became a Gascon, allured by the beauty of the chateau de Lanstrac, a delightful residence owned by his wife. During the last days of the reign of Louis XV., he bought the post of major of the Gate Guards, and lived till 1813, having by great good luck escaped the dangers of the Revolution in the following manner.

Toward the close of the year, 1790, he went to Martinque, where his wife had interests, leaving the management of his property in Gascogne to an honest man, a notary's clerk, named Mathias, who was inclined to - or at any rate did - give into the new ideas. On his return the Comte de Manerville found his possessions intact and well-managed. This sound result was the fruit produced by grafting the Gascon on the Norman.

Madame de Manerville died in 1810. Having learned the importance of worldly goods through the dissipations of his youth, and, giving them, like many another old man, a higher place than they really hold in life, Monsieur de Manerville became increasingly economical, miserly, and sordid. Without reflecting that the avarice of parents prepares the way for the prodigalities of children, he allowed almost nothing to his son, although that son was an only child.

Paul de Manerville, coming home from the college of Vendome in 1810, lived under close paternal discipline for three years. The tyranny by which the old man of seventy oppressed his heir influenced, necessarily, a heart and a character which were not yet formed. Paul, the son, without lacking the physical courage which is vital in the air of Gascony, dared not struggle against his father, and consequently lost that faculty of resistance which begets moral courage. His thwarted feelings were driven to the depths of his heart, where they remained without expression; later, when he felt them to be out of harmony with the maxims of the world, he could only think rightly and act mistakenly. He was capable of fighting for a mere word or look, yet he trembled at the thought of dismissing a servant, - his timidity showing itself in those contests only which required a persistent will. Capable of doing great things to fly from persecution, he would never have prevented it by systematic opposition, nor have faced it with the steady employment of force of will. Timid in thought, bold in actions, he long preserved that inward simplicity which makes a man the dupe and the voluntary victim of things against which certain souls hesitate to revolt, preferring to endure them rather than complain. He was, in point of fact, imprisoned by his father's old mansion, for he had not enough money to consort with young men; he envied their pleasures while unable to share them.

The old gentleman took him every evening, in an old carriage drawn by ill-harnessed old horses, attended by ill-dressed old servants, to royalist houses, where he met a society composed of the relics of the parliamentary nobility and the martial nobility. These two nobilities coalescing after the Revolution, had now transformed themselves into a landed aristocracy. Crushed by the vast and swelling fortunes of the maritime cities, this Faubourg Saint-Germain of Bordeaux responded by lofty disdain to the sumptuous displays of commerce, government administrations, and the military. Too young to understand social distinctions and the necessities underlying the apparent assumption which they create, Paul was bored to death among these ancients, unaware that the connections of his youth would eventually secure to him that aristocratic pre-eminence which Frenchmen will forever desire.

He found some slight compensations for the dulness of these evenings in certain manual exercises which always delight young men, and which his father enjoined upon him. The old gentleman considered that to know the art of fencing and the use of arms, to ride well on horseback, to play tennis, to acquire good manners, - in short, to possess all the frivolous accomplishments of the old nobility, - made a young man of the present day a finished gentleman. Accordingly, Paul took a fencing-lesson every morning, went to the riding-school, and practised in a pistol-gallery. The rest of his time was spent in reading novels, for his father would never have allowed the more abstruse studies now considered necessary to finish an education.

So monotonous a life would soon have killed the poor

youth if the death of the old man had not delivered him from this tyranny at the moment when it was becoming intolerable. Paul found himself in possession of considerable capital, accumulated by his father's avarice, together with landed estates in the best possible condition. But he now held Bordeaux in horror; neither did he like Lanstrac, where his father had taken him to spend the summers, employing his whole time from morning till night in hunting.

As soon as the estate was fairly settled, the young heir, eager for enjoyment, bought consols with his capital, left the management of the landed property to old Mathias, his father's notary, and spent the next six years away from Bordeaux. At first he was attached to the French embassy at Naples; after that he was secretary of legation at Madrid, and then in London, - making in this way the tour of Europe.

After seeing the world and life, after losing several illusions, after dissipating all the loose capital which his father had amassed, there came a time when, in order to continue his way of life, Paul was forced to draw upon the territorial revenues which his notary was laying by. At this critical moment, seized by one of the so-called virtuous impulses, he determined to leave Paris, return to Bordeaux, regulate his affairs, lead the life of a country gentleman at Lanstrac, improve his property, marry, and become, in the end, a deputy.

Paul was a count; nobility was once more of matrimonial value; he could, and he ought to make a good marriage. While many women desire a title, many others like to marry a man to whom a knowledge of life is familiar. Now Paul had acquired, in exchange for the sum of seven hundred thousand francs squandered in six years, that possession, which cannot be bought and is practically of more value than gold and silver; a knowledge which exacts long study, probation, examinations, friends, enemies, acquaintances, certain manners, elegance of form and demeanor, a graceful and euphonious name, - a knowledge, moreover, which means many love-affairs, duels, bets lost on a race-course, disillusions, deceptions, annoyances, toils, and a vast variety of undigested pleasures. In short, he had become what is called elegant. But in spite of his mad extravagance he had never made himself a mere fashionable man. In the burlesque army of men of the world, the man of fashion holds the place of a marshal of France, the man of elegance is the equivalent of a lieutenant-general. Paul enjoyed his lesser reputation, of elegance, and knew well how to sustain it. His servants were well-dressed, his equipages were cited, his suppers had a certain vogue; in short, his bachelor establishment was counted among the seven or eight whose splendor equalled that of the finest houses in Paris.

But - he had not caused the wretchedness of any woman; he gambled without losing; his luck was not notorious; he was far too upright to deceive or mislead any one, no matter who, even a wanton; never did he leave his billets-doux lying about, and he possessed no coffer or desk for love-letters which his friends were at liberty to read while he tied his cravat or trimmed his beard. Moreover, not willing to dip into his Guienne property, he had not that bold extravagance which leads to great strokes and calls attention at any cost to the proceedings of a young man. Neither did he borrow money, but he had the folly to lend to friends, who then deserted him and spoke of him no more either for good or evil. He seemed to have regulated his dissipations methodically. The secret of his character lay in his father's tyranny, which had made him, as it were, a social mongrel.

So, one morning, he said to a friend named de Marsay, who afterwards became celebrated: -

"My dear fellow, life has a meaning."

"You must be twenty-seven years of age before you can find it out," replied de Marsay, laughing.

"Well, I am twenty-seven; and precisely because I am twenty-seven I mean to live the life of a country gentleman at Lanstrac. I'll transport my belongings to Bordeaux into my father's old mansion, and I'll spend three months of the year in Paris in this house, which I shall keep."

"Will you marry?"

"I will marry."

"I'm your friend, as you know, my old Paul," said de Marsay, after a moment's silence, "and I say to you: settle down into a worthy father and husband and you'll be ridiculous for the rest of your days. If you could be happy and ridiculous, the thing might be thought of; but you will not be happy. You haven't a strong enough wrist to drive a household. I'll do you justice and say you are a perfect horseman; no one knows as well as you how to pick up or thrown down the reins, and make a horse prance, and sit firm to the saddle. But, my dear fellow, marriage is another thing. I see you now, led along at a slapping pace by Madame la Comtesse de Manerville, going whither you would not, oftener at a gallop than a trot, and presently unhorsed! - yes, unhorsed into a ditch and your legs broken. Listen to me. You still have some forty-odd thousand francs a year from your property in the Gironde. Good. Take your horses and servants and furnish your house in Bordeaux; you can be king of Bordeaux, you can promulgate there the edicts that we put forth in Paris; you can be the correspondent of our stupidities. Very good. Play the rake in the provinces; better still, commit follies; follies may win you celebrity. But - don't marry. Who marries now-a-days? Only merchants, for the sake of their capital, or to be two to drag the cart; only peasants who want to produce children to work for them; only brokers and notaries who want a wife's 'dot' to pay for their practice; only miserable kings who are forced to continue their miserable dynasties. But we are exempt from the pack, and you want to shoulder it! And why DO you want to marry? You ought to give your best friend your reasons. In the first place, if you marry an heiress as rich as yourself, eighty thousand francs a year for two is not the same thing as forty thousand francs a year for one, because the two are soon three or four when the children come. You haven't surely any love for that silly race of Manerville which would only hamper you? Are you ignorant of what a father and mother have to be? Marriage, my old Paul, is the silliest of all the social immolations; our children alone profit by it, and don't know its price until their horses are nibbling the flowers on our grave. Do you regret your father, that old tyrant who made your first years wretched? How can you be sure that your children will love you? The very care you take of their education, your precautions for their happiness, your necessary sternness will lessen their affection. Children love a weak or a prodigal father, whom they will despise in after years. You'll live betwixt fear and contempt. No man is a good head of a family merely because he wants to be. Look round on all our friends and name to me one whom you would like to have for a son. We have known a good many who dishonor their names. Children, my dear Paul, are the most difficult kind of merchandise to take care of. Yours, you think, will be angels; well, so be it! Have you ever sounded the gulf which lies between the lives of a bachelor and a married man? Listen. As a bachelor you can say to yourself: 'I shall never exhibit more than a certain amount of the ridiculous; the public will think of me what I choose it to think.' Married, you'll drop into the infinitude of the ridiculous! Bachelor, you can make your own happiness; you enjoy some to-day, you do without it to-morrow; married, you must take it as it comes; and the day you want it you will have to go without it. Marry, and you'll grow a blockhead; you'll calculate dowries; you'll talk morality, public and religious; you'll think young men immoral and dangerous; in short, you'll become a social academician. It's pitiable! The old bachelor whose property the heirs are waiting for, who fights to his last breath with his nurse for a spoonful of drink, is blest in comparison with a married man. I'm not speaking of all that will happen to annoy, bore, irritate, coerce, oppose, tyrannize, narcotize, paralyze, and idiotize a man in marriage, in that struggle of two beings always in one another's presence, bound forever, who have coupled each other under the strange impression that they were suited. No, to tell you those things would be merely a repetition of Boileau, and we know him by heart. Still, I'll forgive your absurd idea if you will promise me to marry "en grand seigneur"; to entail your property; to have two legitimate children, to give your wife a house and household absolutely distinct from yours; to meet her only in society, and never to return from a journey without sending her a courier to announce it. Two hundred thousand francs a year will suffice for such a life and your antecedents will enable you to marry some rich English woman hungry for a title. That's an aristocratic life which seems to me thoroughly French; the only life in which we can retain the respect and friendship of a woman; the only life which distinguishes a man from the present crowd, - in short, the only life for which a young man should even think of resigning his bachelor blessings. Thus established, the Comte de Manerville may advise his epoch, place himself above the world, and be nothing less than a minister or an ambassador. Ridicule can never touch him; he has gained the social advantages of marriage while keeping all the privileges of a bachelor."

"But, my good friend, I am not de Marsay; I am plainly, as you yourself do me the honor to say, Paul de Manerville, worthy father and husband, deputy of the Centre, possibly peer of France, - a destiny extremely commonplace; but I am modest and I resign myself."

"Yes, but your wife," said the pitiless de Marsay, "will she resign herself?"

"My wife, my dear fellow, will do as I wish."

"Ah! my poor friend, is that where you are? Adieu, Paul. Henceforth, I refuse to respect you. One word more, however, for I cannot agree coldly to your abdication. Look and see in what the strength of our position lies. A bachelor with only six thousand francs a year remaining to him has at least his reputation for elegance and the memory of success. Well, even that fantastic shadow has enormous value in it. Life still offers many chances to the unmarried man. Yes, he can aim at anything. But marriage, Paul, is the social 'Thus far shalt thou go and no farther.' Once married you can never be anything but what you then are - unless your wife should deign to care for you."

"But," said Paul, "you are crushing me down with exceptional theories. I am tired of living for others; of having horses merely to exhibit them; of doing all things for the sake of what may be said of them; of wasting my substance to keep fools from crying out: 'Dear, dear! Paul is still driving the same carriage. What has he done with his fortune? Does he squander it? Does he gamble at the Bourse? No, he's a millionaire. Madame such a one is mad about him. He sent to England for a harness which is certainly the handsomest in all Paris. The four-horse equipages of Messieurs de Marsay and de Manerville were much noticed at Longchamps; the harness was perfect' - in short, the thousand silly things with which a crowd of idiots lead us by the nose. Believe me, my dear Henri, I admire your power, but I don't envy it. You know how to judge of life; you think and act as a statesman; you are able to place yourself above all ordinary laws, received ideas, adopted conventions, and acknowledged prejudices; in short, you can grasp the profits of a situation in which I should find nothing but ill-luck. Your cool, systematic, possibly true deductions are, to the eyes of the masses, shockingly immoral. I belong to the masses. I must play my game of life according to the rules of the society in which I am forced to live. While putting yourself above all human things on peaks of ice, you still have feelings; but as for me, I should freeze to death. The life of that great majority, to which I belong in my commonplace way, is made up of emotions of which I now have need. Often a man coquets with a dozen women and obtains none. Then, whatever be his strength, his cleverness, his knowledge of the world, he undergoes convulsions, in which he is crushed as between two gates. For my part, I like the peaceful chances and changes of life; I want that wholesome existence in which we find a woman always at our side."

"A trifle indecorous, your marriage!" exclaimed de Marsay.

Paul was not to be put out of countenance, and continued: "Laugh if you like; I shall feel myself a happy man when my valet enters my room in the morning and says: 'Madame is awaiting monsieur for breakfast'; happier still at night, when I return to find a heart -"

"Altogether indecorous, my dear Paul. You are not yet moral enough to marry."

"- a heart in which to confide my interests and my secrets. I wish to live in such close union with a woman that our affection shall not depend upon a yes or a no, or be open to the disillusions of love. In short, I have the necessary courage to become, as you say, a worthy husband and father. I feel myself fitted for family joys; I wish to put myself under the conditions prescribed by society; I desire to have a wife and children."

"You remind me of a hive of honey-bees! But go your way, you'll be a dupe all your life. Ha, ha! you wish to marry to have a wife! In other words, you wish to solve satisfactorily to your own profit the most difficult problem invented by those bourgeois morals which were created by the French Revolution; and, what is more, you mean to begin your attempt by a life of retirement. Do you think your wife won't crave the life you say you despise? Will *she* be disgusted with it, as you are? If you won't accept the noble conjugality just formulated for your benefit by your friend de Marsay, listen, at any rate, to his final advice. Remain a bachelor for the next thirteen years; amuse yourself like a lost soul; then, at forty, on your first attack of gout, marry a widow of thirty-six. Then you may possibly be happy. If you now take a young girl to wife, you'll die a madman."

"Ah ca! tell me why!" cried Paul, somewhat piqued.

"My dear fellow," replied de Marsay, "Boileau's satire against women is a tissue of poetical commonplaces. Why shouldn't women have defects? Why condemn them for having the most obvious thing in human nature? To my mind, the problem of marriage is not at all at the point where Boileau puts it. Do you suppose that marriage is the same thing as love, and that being a man suffices to make a wife love you? Have you gathered nothing in your boudoir experience but pleasant memories? I tell you that everything in our bachelor life leads to fatal errors in the married man unless he is a profound observer of the human heart. In the happy days of his youth a man, by the caprice of our customs, is always lucky; he triumphs over women who are all ready to be triumphed over and who obey their own desires. One thing after another - the obstacles created by the laws, the sentiments and natural defences of women - all engender a mutuality of sensations which deceives superficial persons as to their future relations in marriage, where obstacles no longer exist, where the wife submits to love instead of permitting it, and frequently repulses pleasure instead of desiring it. Then, the whole aspect of a man's life changes. The bachelor, who is free and without a care, need never fear repulsion; in marriage, repulsion is almost certain and irreparable. It may be possible for a lover to make a woman reverse an unfavorable decision, but such a change, my dear Paul, is the Waterloo of husbands. Like Napoleon, the husband is thenceforth condemned to victories which, in spite of their number, do not prevent the first defeat from crushing him. The woman, so flattered by the perseverance, so delighted with the ardor of a lover, calls the same things brutality in a husband. You, who talk of marrying, and who will marry, have you ever meditated on the Civil Code? I myself have never muddied my feet in that hovel of commentators, that garret of gossip, called the Law-school. I have never so much as opened the Code; but I see its application on the vitals of society. The Code, my dear Paul, makes woman a ward; it considers her a child, a minor. Now how must we govern children? By fear. In that one word, Paul, is the curb of the beast. Now, feel your own pulse! Have you the strength to play the tyrant, - you, so gentle, so kind a friend, so confiding; you, at whom I have laughed, but whom I love, and love enough to reveal to you my science? For this is science. Yes, it proceeds from a science which the Germans are already calling Anthropology. Ah! if I had not already solved the mystery of life by pleasure, if I had not a profound antipathy for those who think instead of act, if I did not despise the ninnies who are silly enough to believe in the truth of a book, when the sands of the African deserts are made of the ashes of I know not how many unknown and pulverized

Londons, Romes, Venices, and Parises, I would write a book on modern marriages made under the influence of the Christian system, and I'd stick a lantern on that heap of sharp stones among which lie the votaries of the social 'multiplicamini.' But the question is, Does humanity require even an hour of my time? And besides, isn't the more reasonable use of ink that of snaring hearts by writing love-letters? - Well, shall you bring the Comtesse de Manerville here, and let us see her?"

"Perhaps," said Paul.

"We shall still be friends," said de Marsay.

"If - " replied Paul.

"Don't be uneasy; we will treat you politely, as Maison-Rouge treated the English at Fontenoy."

CHAPTER II

THE PINK OF FASHION

Though the foregoing conversation affected the Comte de Manerville somewhat, he made it a point of duty to carry out his intentions, and he returned to Bordeaux during the winter of the year 1821.

The expenses he incurred in restoring and furnishing his family mansion sustained the reputation for elegance which had preceded him. Introduced through his former connections to the royalist society of Bordeaux, to which he belonged as much by his personal opinions as by his name and fortune, he soon obtained a fashionable pre-eminence. His knowledge of life, his manners, his Parisian acquirements enchanted the Faubourg Saint-Germain of Bordeaux. An old marquise made use of a term formerly in vogue at court to express the flowery beauty of the fops and beaux of the olden time, whose language and demeanor were social laws: she called him "the pink of fashion." The liberal clique caught up the word and used it satirically as a nickname, while the royalist party continued to employ it in good faith.

Paul de Manerville acquitted himself gloriously of the obligations imposed by his flowery title. It happened to him, as to many a mediocre actor, that the day when the public granted him their full attention he became, one may almost say, superior. Feeling at his ease, he displayed the fine qualities which accompanied his defects. His wit had nothing sharp or bitter in it; his manners were not supercilious; his intercourse with women expressed the respect they like, - it was neither too deferential, nor too familiar; his foppery went no farther than a care for his personal appearance which made him agreeable; he showed consideration for rank; he allowed young men a certain freedom, to which his Parisian experience assigned due limits; though skilful with sword and pistol, he was noted for a feminine gentleness for which others were grateful. His medium height and plumpness (which had not yet increased into obesity, an obstacle to personal elegance) did not prevent his outer man from playing the part of a Bordelais Brummell. A white skin tinged with the hues of health, handsome hands and feet, blue eyes with long lashes, black hair, graceful motions, a chest voice which kept to its middle tones and vibrated in the listener's heart, harmonized well with his sobriquet. Paul was indeed that delicate flower which needs such careful culture, the qualities of which display themselves only in a moist and suitable soil, - a flower which rough treatment dwarfs, which the hot sun burns, and a frost lays low. He was one of those men made to receive happiness, rather than to give it; who have something of the woman in their nature, wishing to be divined, understood, encouraged; in short, a man to whom conjugal love ought to come as a providence.

If such a character creates difficulties in private life, it is gracious and full of attraction for the world. Consequently, Paul had great success in the narrow social circle of the provinces, where his mind, always, so to speak, in half-tints, was better appreciated than in Paris.

The arrangement of his house and the restoration of the chateau de Lanstrac, where he introduced the comfort and luxury of an English country-house, absorbed the capital saved by the notary during the preceding six years. Reduced now to his strict income of forty-odd thousand a year, he thought himself wise and prudent in so regulating his household as not to exceed it.

After publicly exhibiting his equipages, entertaining the most distinguished young men of the place, and giving various hunting parties on the estate at Lanstrac, Paul saw very plainly that provincial life would never do without marriage. Too young to employ his time in miserly occupations, or in trying to interest himself in the speculative improvements in which provincials sooner or later engage (compelled thereto by the necessity of establishing their children), he soon felt the need of that variety of distractions a habit of which becomes at last the very life of a Parisian. A name to preserve, property to transmit to heirs, social relations to be created by a household where the principal families of the neighborhood could assemble, and a weariness of all irregular connections, were not, however, the determining reasons of his matrimonial desires. From the time he first returned to the provinces he had been secretly in love with the queen of Bordeaux, the great beauty, Mademoiselle Evangelista.

About the beginning of the century, a rich Spaniard, named Evangelista, established himself in Bordeaux, where his letters of recommendation, as well as his large fortune, gave him an entrance to the salons of the nobility. His wife contributed greatly to maintain him in the good graces of an aristocracy which may perhaps have adopted him in the first instance merely to pique the society of the class below them. Madame Evangelista, who belonged to the Casa-Reale, an illustrious family of Spain, was a Creole, and, like all women served by slaves, she lived as a great lady, knew nothing of the value of money, repressed no whims, even the most expensive, finding them ever satisfied by an adoring husband who generously concealed from her knowledge the running-gear of the financial machine. Happy in finding her pleased with Bordeaux, where his interests obliged him to live, the Spaniard bought a house, set up a household, received in much style, and gave many proofs of possessing a fine taste in all things. Thus, from 1800 to 1812, Monsieur and Madame Evangelista were objects of great interest to the community of Bordeaux.

The Spaniard died in 1813, leaving his wife a widow at thirty-two years of age, with an immense fortune and the prettiest little girl in the world, a child of eleven, who promised to be, and did actually become, a most accomplished young woman. Clever as Madame Evangelista was, the Restoration altered her position; the royalist party cleared its ranks and several of the old families left Bordeaux. Though the head and hand of her husband were lacking in the direction of her affairs, for which she had hitherto shown the indifference of a Creole and the inaptitude of a lackadaisical woman, she was determined to make no change in her manner of living. At the period when Paul resolved to return to his native town, Mademoiselle Natalie Evangelista was a remarkably beautiful young girl, and, apparently, the richest match in Bordeaux, where the steady diminution of her mother's capital was unknown. In order to prolong her reign, Madame Evangelista had squandered enormous sums. Brilliant fetes and the continuation of an almost regal style of living kept the public in its past belief as to the wealth of the Spanish family.

Natalie was now in her nineteenth year, but no proposal of marriage had as yet reached her mother's ear. Accustomed to gratify her fancies, Mademoiselle Evangelista wore cashmeres and jewels, and lived in a style of luxury which alarmed all speculative suitors in a region and at a period when sons were as calculating as their parents. The fatal remark, "None but a prince can afford to marry Mademoiselle Evangelista," circulated among the salons and the cliques. Mothers of families, dowagers who had granddaughters to establish, young girls jealous of Natalie, whose elegance and tyrannical beauty annoyed them, took pains to envenom this opinion with treacherous remarks. When they heard a possible suitor say with ecstatic admiration, as Natalie entered a ball-room, "Heavens, how beautiful she is!" "Yes," the mammas would answer, "but expensive." If some new-comer thought Mademoiselle Evangelista bewitching and said to a marriageable man that he couldn't do it better, "Who would be bold enough," some woman would reply, "to marry a girl whose mother gives her a thousand francs a month for her toilet, - a girl who has horses and a maid of her own, and wears laces? Yes, her 'peignoirs' are trimmed with mechlin. The price of her washing would support the household of a clerk. She wears pelerines in the morning which actually cost six francs to get up."

These, and other speeches said occasionally in the form of praise extinguished the desires that some men might have had to marry the beautiful Spanish girl.

Queen of every ball, accustomed to flattery, "blasee" with the smiles and the admiration which followed her every step, Natalie, nevertheless, knew nothing of life. She lived as the bird which flies, as the flower that blooms, finding every one about her eager to do her will. She was ignorant of the price of things; she knew neither the value of money, nor whence it came, how it should be managed, and how spent. Possibly she thought that every household had cooks and coachmen, lady's-maids and footmen, as the fields have hay and the trees their fruits. To her, beggars and paupers, fallen trees and waste lands seemed in the same category. Pampered and petted as her mother's hope, no fatigue was allowed to spoil her pleasure. Thus she bounded through life as a courser on his steppe, unbridled and unshod.

Six month's after Paul's arrival the Pink of Fashion and the Queen of Balls met in presence of the highest society of the town of Bordeaux. The two flowers looked at each other with apparent coldness, and mutually thought each other charming. Interested in watching the effects of the meeting, Madame Evangelista divined in the expression of Paul's eyes the feelings within him, and she muttered to herself, "He will be my son-in-law." Paul, on the other hand, said to himself, as he looked at Natalie, "She will be my wife."

The wealth of the Evangelistas, proverbial in Bordeaux, had remained in Paul's mind as a memory of his childhood. Thus the pecuniary conditions were known to him from the start, without necessitating those discussions and inquiries which are as repugnant to a timid mind as to a proud one. When some persons attempting to say to Paul a few flattering phrases as to

Natalie's manner, language, and beauty, ending by remarks, cruelly calculated to deter him, on the lavish extravagance of the Evangelistas, the Pink of Fashion replied with a disdain that was well-deserved by such provincial pettiness. This method of receiving such speeches soon silenced them; for he now set the tone to the ideas and language as well as to the manners of those about him. He had imported from his travels a certain development of the Britannic personality with its icy barriers, also a tone of Byronic pessimism as to life, together with English plate, boot-polish, ponies, yellow gloves, cigars, and the habit of galloping.

It thus happened that Paul escaped the discouragements hitherto presented to marriageable men by dowagers and young girls. Madame Evangelista began by asking him to formal dinners on various occasions. The Pink of Fashion would not, of course, miss festivities to which none but the most distinguished young men of the town were bidden. In spite of the coldness that Paul assumed, which deceived neither mother nor daughter, he was drawn, step by step, into the path of marriage. Sometimes as he passed in his tilbury, or rode by on his fine English horse, he heard the young men of his acquaintance say to one another: -

"There's a lucky man. He is rich and handsome, and is to marry, so they say, Mademoiselle Evangelista. There are some men for whom the world seems made."

When he met the Evangelistas he felt proud of the particular distinction which mother and daughter imparted to their bows. If Paul had not secretly, within his heart, fallen in love with Mademoiselle Natalie, society would certainly have married him to her in spite of himself. Society, which never causes good, is the accomplice of much evil; then when it beholds the evil it has hatched maternally, it rejects and revenges it. Society in Bordeaux, attributing a "dot" of a million to Mademoiselle Evangelista, bestowed it upon Paul without awaiting the consent of either party. Their fortunes, so it was said, agreed as well as their persons. Paul had the same habits of luxury and elegance in the midst of which Natalie had been brought up. He had just arranged for himself a house such as no other man in Bordeaux could have offered her. Accustomed to Parisian expenses and the caprices of Parisian women, he alone was fitted to meet the pecuniary difficulties which were likely to follow this marriage with a girl who was as much of a Creole and a great lady as her mother. Where they themselves, remarked the marriageable men, would have been ruined, the Comte de Manerville, rich as he was, could evade disaster. In short, the marriage was made. Persons in the highest royalist circles said a few engaging words to Paul which flattered his vanity: -

"Every one gives you Mademoiselle Evangelista. If you marry her you will do well. You could not find, even in Paris, a more delightful girl. She is beautiful, graceful, elegant, and takes after the Casa-Reales through her mother. You will make a charming couple; you have the same tastes, the same desires in life, and you will certainly have the most agreeable house in Bordeaux. Your wife need only bring her night-cap; all is ready for her. You are fortunate indeed in such a mother-in-law. A woman of intelligence, and very adroit, she will be a great help to you in public life, to which you ought to aspire. Besides, she has sacrificed everything to her daughter, whom she adores, and Natalie will, no doubt, prove a good wife, for she loves her mother. You must soon bring the matter to a conclusion."

"That is all very well," replied Paul, who, in spite of his love, was desirous of keeping his freedom of action, "but I must be sure that the conclusion shall be a happy one."

He now went frequently to Madame Evangelista's, partly to occupy his vacant hours, which were harder for him to employ than for most men. There alone he breathed the atmosphere of grandeur and luxury to which he was accustomed.

At forty years of age, Madame Evangelista was beautiful, with the beauty of those glorious summer sunsets which crown a cloudless day. Her spotless reputation had given an endless topic of conversation to the Bordeaux cliques; the curiosity of the women was all the more lively because the widow gave signs of the temperament which makes a Spanish woman and a Creole particularly noted. She had black eyes and hair, the feet and form of a Spanish woman, - that swaying form the movements of which have a name in Spain. Her face, still beautiful, was particularly seductive for its Creole complexion, the vividness of which can be described only by comparing it to muslin overlying crimson, so equally is the whiteness suffused with color. Her figure, which was full and rounded, attracted the eye by a grace which united nonchalance with vivacity, strength with ease. She attracted and she imposed, she seduced, but promised nothing. She was tall, which gave her at times the air and carriage of a queen. Men were taken by her conversation like birds in a snare; for she had by nature that genius which necessity bestows on schemes; she advanced from concession to concession, strengthening herself with what she gained to ask for more, knowing well how to retreat with rapid steps when concessions were demanded in return. Though ignorant of facts, she had known the courts of Spain and Naples, the celebrated men of the two Americas, many illustrious families of England and the continent, all of which gave her so extensive an education superficially that it seemed immense. She received her society with the grace and dignity which are never learned, but which come to certain naturally fine spirits like a second nature; assimilating choice things wherever they are met. If her reputation for virtue was unexplained, it gave at any rate much authority to her actions, her conversation, and her character.

Mother and daughter had a true friendship for each other, beyond the filial and maternal sentiment. They suited one another, and their perpetual contact had never produced the slightest jar. Consequently many persons explained Madame Evangelista's actions by maternal love. But although Natalie consoled her mother's persistent widowhood, she may not have been the only motive for it. Madame Evangelista had been, it was said, in love with a man who recovered his titles and property under the Restoration. This man, desirous of marrying her in 1814 had discreetly severed the connection in 1816. Madame Evangelista, to all appearance the best-hearted woman in the world, had, in the depths of her nature, a fearful quality, explainable only by Catherine de Medici's device: "Odiate e aspettate" - "Hate and wait." Accustomed to rule, having always been obeyed, she was like other royalties, amiable, gentle, easy and pleasant in ordinary life, but terrible, implacable, if the pride of the woman, the Spaniard, and the Casa-Reale was touched. She never forgave. This woman believed in the power of her hatred; she made an evil fate of it and bade it hover above her enemy. This fatal power she employed against the man who had jilted her. Events which seemed to prove the influence of her "jettatura" - the casting of an evil eye - confirmed her superstitious faith in herself. Though a minister and peer of France, this man began to ruin himself, and soon came to total ruin. His property, his personal and public honor were doomed to perish. At this crisis Madame Evangelista in her brilliant equipage passed her faithless lover walking on foot in the Champes Elysees, and crushed him with a look which flamed with triumph. This misadventure, which occupied her mind for two years, was the original cause of her not remarrying. Later, her pride had drawn comparisons between the suitors who presented themselves and the husband who had loved her so sincerely and so well.

She had thus reached, through mistaken calculations and disappointed hopes, that period of life when women have no other part to take in life than that of mother; a part which involves the sacrifice of themselves to their children, the placing of their interests outside of self upon another household, - the last refuge of human affections.

Madame Evangelista divined Paul's nature intuitively, and hid her own from his perception. Paul was the very man she desired for a son-in-law, for the responsible editor of her future power. He belonged, through his mother, to the family of Maulincour, and the old Baronne de Maulincour, the friend of the Vidame de Pamiers, was then living in the centre of the faubourg Saint-Germain. The grandson of the baroness, Auguste de Maulincour, held a fine position in the army. Paul would therefore be an excellent introducer for the Evangelistas into Parisian society. The widow had known something of the Paris of the Empire, she now desired to shine in the Paris of the Restoration. There alone were the elements of political fortune, the only business in which women of the world could decently co-operate. Madame Evangelista, compelled by her husband's affairs to reside in Bordeaux, disliked the place. She desired a wider field, as gamblers rush to higher stakes. For her own personal ends, therefore, she looked to Paul as a means of destiny, she proposed to employ the resources of her own talent and knowledge of life to advance her son-in-law, in order to enjoy through him the delights of power. Many men are thus made the screens of secret feminine ambitions. Madame Evangelista had, however, more than one interest, as we shall see, in laying hold of her daughter's husband.

Paul was naturally captivated by this woman, who charmed him all the more because she seemed to seek no influence over him. In reality she was using her ascendancy to magnify herself, her daughter, and all her surroundings in his eyes, for the purpose of ruling from the start the man in whom she saw a means of gratifying her social longings. Paul, on the other hand, began to value himself more highly when he felt himself appreciated by the mother and daughter. He thought himself much cleverer than he really was when he found his reflections and sayings accepted and understood by Mademoiselle Natalie - who raised her head and smiled in response to them - and by the mother, whose flattery always seemed involuntary. The two women were so kind and friendly to him, he was so sure of pleasing them, they ruled him so delightfully by holding the thread of his self-love, that he soon passed all his time at the hotel Evangelista.

A year after his return to Bordeaux, Comte Paul, without having declared himself, was so attentive to Natalie that the world considered him as courting her. Neither mother nor daughter appeared to be thinking of marriage. Mademoiselle Evangelista preserved towards Paul the reserve of a great lady who can make herself charming and converse agreeably without permitting a single step into intimacy. This reserve, so little customary among provincials, pleased Paul immensely. Timid men are shy; sudden proposals alarm them. They retreat from happiness when it comes with a rush, and accept misfortune if it presents itself mildly with gentle shadows. Paul therefore committed himself in his own mind all the more because he saw no effort on Madame Evangelista's part to bind him. She fairly seduced him one evening by remarking that to superior women as well as men there came a period of life when ambition superseded all the earlier emotions of life.

"That woman is fitted," thought Paul, as he left her, "to advance me in diplomacy before I am even made a deputy."

If, in all the circumstances of life a man does not turn over and over both things and ideas in order to examine them thoroughly under their different aspects before taking action, that man is weak and incomplete and in danger of fatal failure. At this moment Paul was an optimist; he saw everything to advantage, and did not tell himself than an ambitious mother-in-law might prove a tyrant. So, every evening as he left the house, he fancied himself a married man, allured his mind with its own thought, and slipped on the slippers of wedlock cheerfully. In the first place, he had enjoyed his freedom too long to regret the loss of it; he was tired of a bachelor's life, which offered him nothing new; he now saw only its annoyances; whereas if he thought at times of the difficulties of marriage, its pleasures, in which lay novelty, came far more prominently before his mind.

"Marriage," he said to himself, "is disagreeable for people without means, but half its troubles disappear before wealth."

Every day some favorable consideration swelled the advantages which he now saw in this particular alliance.

"No matter to what position I attain, Natalie will always be on the level of her part," thought he, "and that is no small merit in a woman. How many of the Empire men I've seen who suffered horribly through their wives! It is a great condition of happiness not to feel one's pride or one's vanity wounded by the companion we have chosen. A man can never be really unhappy with a well-bred wife; she will never make him ridiculous; such a woman is certain to be useful to him. Natalie will receive in her own house admirably."

So thinking, he taxed his memory as to the most distinguished women of the faubourg Saint-Germain, in order to convince himself that Natalie could, if not eclipse them, at any rate stand among them on a footing of perfect equality. All comparisons were to her advantage, for they rested on his own imagination, which followed his desires. Paris would have shown him daily other natures, young girls of other styles of beauty and charm, and the multiplicity of impressions would have balanced his mind; whereas in Bordeaux Natalie had no rivals, she was the solitary flower; moreover, she appeared to him at a moment when Paul was under the tyranny of an idea to which most men succumb at his age.

Thus these reasons of propinquity, joined to reasons of self-love and a real passion which had no means of satisfaction except by marriage, led Paul on to an irrational love, which he had, however, the good sense to keep to himself. He even endeavored to study Mademoiselle Evangelista as a man should who desires not to compromise his future life; for the words of his friend de Marsay did sometimes rumble in his ears like a warning. But, in the first place, persons accustomed to luxury have a certain indifference to it which misleads them. They despise it, they use it; it is an instrument, and not the object of their existence. Paul never imagined, as he observed the habits of life of the two ladies, that they covered a gulf of ruin. Then, though there may exist some general rules to soften the asperities of marriage, there are none by which they can be accurately foreseen and evaded. When trouble arises between two persons who have undertaken to render life agreeable and easy to each other, it comes from the contact of continual intimacy, which, of course, does not exist between young people before they marry, and will never exist so long as our present social laws and customs prevail in France. All is more or less deception between the two young persons about to take each other for life, - an innocent and involuntary deception, it is true. Each endeavors to appear in a favorable light; both take a tone and attitude conveying a more favorable idea of their nature than they are able to maintain in after years.

Real life, like the weather, is made up of gray and cloudy days alternating with those when the sun shines and the fields are gay. Young people, however, exhibit fine weather and no clouds. Later they attribute to marriage the evils inherent in life itself; for there is in man a disposition to lay the blame of his own misery on the persons and things that surround him.

To discover in the demeanor, or the countenance, or the words, or the gestures of Mademoiselle Evangelista any indication that revealed the imperfections of her character, Paul must have possessed not only the knowledge of Lavater and Gall, but also a science in which there exists no formula of doctrine, - the individual and personal science of an observer, which, for its perfection, requires an almost universal knowledge. Natalie's face, like that of most young girls, was impenetrable. The deep, serene peace given by sculptors to the virgin faces of Justice and Innocence, divinities aloof from all earthly agitations, is the greatest charm of a young girl, the sign of her purity. Nothing, as yet, has stirred her; no shattered passion, no hope betrayed has clouded the placid expression of that pure face. Is that expression assumed? If so, there is no young girl behind it.

Natalie, closely held to the heart of her mother, had received, like other Spanish women, an education that was solely religious, together with a few instructions from her mother as to the part in life she was called upon to play. Consequently, the calm, untroubled expression of her face was natural. And yet it formed a casing in which the woman was wrapped as the moth in its cocoon. Nevertheless, any man clever at handling the scalpel of analysis might have detected in Natalie certain indications of the difficulties her character would present when brought into contact with conjugal or social life. Her beauty, which was really marvellous, came from extreme regularity of feature harmonizing with the proportions of the head and the body. This species of perfection augurs ill for the mind; and there are few exceptions to the rule. All superior nature is found to have certain slight imperfections of form which become irresistible attractions, luminous points from which shine vivid sentiments, and on which the eye rests gladly. Perfect harmony expresses usually the coldness of a mixed organization.

Natalie's waist was round, - a sign of strength, but also the infallible indication of a will which becomes obstinacy in persons whose mind is neither keen nor broad. Her hands, like those of a Greek statue, confirmed the predictions of face and figure by revealing an inclination for illogical domination, of willing for will's sake only. Her eyebrows met, - a sign, according to some observers, which indicates jealousy. The jealousy of superior minds becomes emulation and leads to great things; that of small minds turns to hatred. The "hate and wait" of her mother was in her nature, without disguise. Her eyes were black apparently, though really brown with orange streaks, contrasting with her hair, of the ruddy tint so prized by the Romans, called auburn in England, a color which often appears in the offspring of persons of jet black hair, like that of Monsieur and Madame Evangelista. The whiteness and delicacy of Natalie's complexion gave to the contrast of color in her eyes and hair an inexpressible charm; and yet it was a charm that was purely external; for whenever the lines of a face are lacking in a certain soft roundness, whatever may be the finish and grace of the details, the beauty therein expressed is not of the soul. These roses of deceptive youth will drop their leaves, and you will be surprised in a few years to see hardness and dryness where you once admired what seemed to be the beauty of noble qualities.

Though the outlines of Natalie's face had something august about them, her chin was slightly "empate," - a painter's expression which will serve to show the existence of sentiments the violence of which would only become manifest in after life. Her mouth, a trifle drawn in, expressed a haughty pride in keeping with her hand, her chin, her brows, and her beautiful figure. And - as a last diagnostic to guide the judgment of a connoisseur - Natalie's pure voice, a most seductive voice, had certain metallic tones. Softly as that brassy ring was managed, and in spite of the grace with which its sounds ran through the compass of the voice, that organ revealed the character of the Duke of Alba, from whom the Casa-Reales were collaterally descended. These indications were those of violent passions without tenderness, sudden devotions, irreconcilable dislikes, a mind without intelligence, and the desire to rule natural to persons who feel themselves inferior to their pretensions.

These defects, born of temperament and constitution, were buried in Natalie like ore in a mine, and would only appear under the shocks and harsh treatment to which all characters are subjected in this world. Meantime the grace and freshness of her youth, the distinction of her manners, her sacred ignorance, and the sweetness of a young girl, gave a delicate glamour to her features which could not fail to mislead an unthinking or superficial mind. Her mother had early taught her the trick of agreeable talk which appears to imply superiority, replying to arguments by clever jests, and attracting by the graceful volubility beneath which a woman hides the subsoil of her mind, as Nature disguises her barren strata beneath a wealth of ephemeral vegetation. Natalie had the charm of children who have never known what it is to suffer. She charmed by her frankness, and had none of that solemn air which mothers impose on their daughters by laying down a programme of behavior and language until the time comes when they marry and are emancipated. She was gay and natural, like any young girl who knows nothing of marriage, expects only pleasure from it, replies to all objections with a jest, foresees no troubles, and thinks she is acquiring the right to have her own way.

How could Paul, who loved as men love when desire increases love, perceive in a girl of this nature whose beauty dazzled him, the woman, such as she would probably be at thirty, when observers themselves have been misled by these appearances? Besides, if happiness might prove difficult to find in a marriage with such a girl, it was not impossible. Through these embryo defects shone several fine qualities. There is no good quality which, if properly developed by the hand of an able master, will not stifle defects, especially in a young girl who loves him. But to render ductile so intractable a woman, the iron wrist, about which de Marsay had preached to Paul, was needful. The Parisian dandy was right. Fear, inspired by love is an infallible instrument by which to manage the minds of women. Whoso loves, fears; whoso fears is nearer to affection than to hatred.

Had Paul the coolness, firmness, and judgment required for this struggle, which an able husband ought not to let the wife suspect? Did Natalie love Paul? Like most young girls, Natalie mistook for love the first emotions of instinct and the pleasure she felt in Paul's external appearance; but she knew nothing of the things of marriage nor the demands of a home. To her, the Comte de Manerville, a rising diplomatist, to whom the courts of Europe were known, and one of the most elegant young men in Paris, could not seem, what perhaps he was, an ordinary man, without moral force, timid, though brave in some ways, energetic perhaps in adversity, but helpless against the vexations and annoyances that hinder happiness. Would she, in after years, have sufficient tact and insight to distinguish Paul's noble qualities in the midst of his minor defects? Would she not magnify the latter and forget the former, after the manner of young wives who know nothing of life? There comes a time when wives will pardon defects in the husband who spares her annoyances, considering annoyances in the same category as misfortunes. What conciliating power, what wise experience would uphold and enlighten the home of this young pair? Paul and his wife would doubtless think they loved when they had really not advanced beyond the endearments and compliments of the honeymoon. Would Paul in that early period yield to the tyranny of his wife, instead of establishing his empire? Could Paul say, "No?" All was peril to a man so weak where even a strong man ran some risks.

The subject of this Study is not the transition of a bachelor into a married man, - a picture which, if broadly composed, would not lack the attraction which the inner struggles of our nature and feelings give to the commonest situations in life. The events and the ideas which led to the marriage of Paul with Natalie Evangelista are an introduction to our real subject, which is to sketch the great comedy that precedes, in

France, all conjugal pairing. This Scene, until now singularly neglected by our dramatic authors, although it offers novel resources to their wit, controlled Paul's future life and was now awaited by Madame Evangelista with feelings of terror. We mean the discussion which takes place on the subject of the marriage contract in all families, whether noble or bourgeois, for human passions are as keenly excited by small interests as by large ones. These comedies, played before a notary, all resemble, more or less, the one we shall now relate, the interest of which will be far less in the pages of this book than in the memories of married persons.

CHAPTER III

THE MARRIAGE CONTRACT - FIRST DAY

At the beginning of the winter of 1822, Paul de Manerville made a formal request, through his great-aunt, the Baronne de Maulincour, for the hand of Mademoiselle Natalie Evangelista. Though the baroness never stayed more than two months in Medoc, she remained on this occasion till the last of October, in order to assist her nephew through the affair and play the part of a mother to him. After conveying the first suggestions to Madame Evangelista the experienced old woman returned to inform Paul of the results of the overture.

"My child," she said, "the affair is won. In talking of property, I found that Madame Evangelista gives nothing of her own to her daughter. Mademoiselle Natalie's dowry is her patrimony. Marry her, my dear boy. Men who have a name and an estate to transmit, a family to continue, must, sooner or later, end in marriage. I wish I could see my dear Auguste taking that course. You can now carry on the marriage without me; I have nothing to give you but my blessing, and women as old as I are out of place at a wedding. I leave for Paris to-morrow. When you present your wife in society I shall be able to see her and assist her far more to the purpose than now. If you had had no house in Paris I would gladly have arranged the second floor of mine for you."

"Dear aunt," said Paul, "I thank you heartily. But what do you mean when you say that the mother gives nothing of her own, and that the daughter's dowry is her patrimony?"

"The mother, my dear boy, is a sly cat, who takes advantage of her daughter's beauty to impose conditions and allow you only that which she cannot prevent you from having; namely, the daughter's fortune from her father. We old people know the importance of inquiring closely, What has he? What has she? I advise you therefore to give particular instructions to your notary. The marriage contract, my dear child, is the most sacred of all duties. If your father and your mother had not made their bed properly you might now be sleeping without sheets. You will have children, they are the commonest result of marriage, and you must think of them. Consult Maitre Mathias our old notary."

Madame de Maulincour departed, having plunged Paul into a state of extreme perplexity. His mother-in-law a sly cat! Must he struggle for his interests in the marriage contract? Was it necessary to defend them? Who was likely to attack them?

He followed the advice of his aunt and confided the drawing-up of the marriage contract to Maitre Mathias. But these threatened discussions oppressed him, and he went to see Madame Evangelista and announce his intentions in a state of rather lively agitation. Like all timid men, he shrank from allowing the distrust his aunt had put into his mind to be seen; in fact, he considered it insulting. To avoid even a slight jar with a person so imposing to his mind as his future mother-in-law, he proceeded to state his intentions with the circumlocution natural to persons who dare not face a difficulty.

"Madame," he said, choosing a moment when Natalie was absent from the room, "you know, of course, what a family notary is. Mine is a worthy old man, to whom it would be a sincere grief if he were not entrusted with the drawing of my marriage contract."

"Why, of course!" said Madame Evangelista, interrupting him, "but are not marriage contracts always made by agreement of the notaries of both families?"

The time that Paul took to reply to this question was occupied by Madame Evangelista in asking herself, "What is he thinking of?" for women possess in an eminent degree the art of reading thoughts from the play of countenance. She divined the instigations of the great-aunt in the embarrassed glance and the agitated tone of voice which betrayed an inward struggle in Paul's mind.

"At last," she thought to herself, "the fatal day has come; the crisis begins - how will it end? My notary is Monsieur Solonet," she said, after a pause. "Yours, I think you said, is Monsieur Mathias; I will invite them to dinner to-morrow, and they can come to an understanding then. It is their business to conciliate our interests without our interference; just as good cooks are expected to furnish good food without instructions."

"Yes, you are right," said Paul, letting a faint sigh of relief escape from him.

By a singular transposition of parts, Paul, innocent of all wrong-doing, trembled, while Madame Evangelista, though a prey to the utmost anxiety, was outwardly calm.

The widow owed her daughter one-third of the fortune left by Monsieur Evangelista, - namely, nearly twelve hundred thousand francs, - and she knew herself unable to pay it, even by taking the whole of her property to do so. She would therefore be placed at the mercy of a son-in-law. Though she might be able to control Paul if left to himself, would he, when enlightened by his notary, agree to release her from rendering her account as guardian of her daughter's patrimony? If Paul withdrew his proposals all Bordeaux would know the reason and Natalie's future marriage would be made impossible. This mother, who desired the happiness of her daughter, this woman, who from infancy had lived honorably, was aware that on the morrow she must become dishonest. Like those great warriors who fain would blot from their lives the moment when they had felt a secret cowardice, she ardently desired to cut this inevitable day from the record of hers. Most assuredly some hairs on her head must have whitened during the night, when, face to face with facts, she bitterly regretted her extravagance as she felt the hard necessities of the situation.

Among these necessities was that of confiding the truth to her notary, for whom she sent in the morning as soon as she rose. She was forced to reveal to him a secret defaulting she had never been willing to admit to herself, for she had steadily advanced to the abyss, relying on some chance accident, which never happened, to relieve her. There rose in her soul a feeling against Paul, that was neither dislike, nor aversion, nor anything, as yet, unkind; but HE was the cause of this crisis; the opposing party in this secret suit; he became, without knowing it, an innocent enemy she was forced to conquer. What human being did ever yet love his or her dupe? Compelled to deceive and trick him if she could, the Spanish woman resolved, like other women, to put her whole force of character into the struggle, the dishonor of which could be absolved by victory only.

In the stillness of the night she excused her conduct to her own mind by a tissue of arguments in which her pride predominated. Natalie had shared the benefit of her extravagance. There was not a single base or ignoble motive in what she had done. She was no accountant, but was that a crime, a delinquency? A man was only too lucky to obtain a wife like Natalie without a penny. Such a treasure bestowed upon him might surely release her from a guardianship account. How many men had bought the women they loved by greater sacrifices? Why should a man do less for a wife than for a mistress? Besides, Paul was a nullity, a man of no force, incapable; she would spend the best resources of her mind upon him and open to him a fine career; he should owe his future power and position to her influence; in that way she could pay her debt. He would indeed be a fool to refuse such a future; and for what? a few paltry thousands, more or less. He would be infamous if he withdrew for such a reason.

"But," she added, to herself, "if the negotiation does not succeed at once, I shall leave Bordeaux. I can still find a good marriage for Natalie by investing the proceeds of what is left, house and diamonds and furniture, - keeping only a small income for myself."

When a strong soul constructs a way of ultimate escape, - as Richelieu did at Brouage, - and holds in reserve a vigorous end, the resolution becomes a lever which strengthens its immediate way. The thought of this finale in case of failure comforted Madame Evangelista, who fell asleep with all the more confidence as she remembered her assistance in the coming duel.

This was a young man named Solonet, considered the ablest notary in Bordeaux; now twenty-seven years of age and decorated with the Legion of honor for having actively contributed to the second return of the Bourbons. Proud and happy to be received in the home of Madame Evangelista, less as a notary than as belonging to the royalist society of Bordeaux, Solonet had conceived for that fine setting sun one of those passions which women like Madame Evangelista repulse, although flattered and graciously allowing them to exist upon the surface. Solonet remained therefore in a self-satisfied condition of hope and becoming respect. Being sent for, he arrived the next morning with the promptitude of a slave and was received by the coquettish widow in her bedroom, where she allowed him to find her in a very becoming dishabille.

"Can I," she said, "count upon your discretion and your entire devotion in a discussion which will take place in my house this evening? You will readily understand that it relates to the marriage of my daughter."

The young man expended himself in gallant protestations.

"Now to the point," she said.

"I am listening," he replied, checking his ardor.

Madame Evangelista then stated her position baldly.

"My dear lady, that is nothing to be troubled about," said Maitre Solonet, assuming a confident air as soon as his client had given him the exact figures. "The question is how have you conducted yourself toward Monsieur de Manerville? In this matter questions of manner and deportment are of greater importance than those of law and finance."

Madame Evangelista wrapped herself in dignity. The notary learned to his satisfaction that until the present moment his client's relations to Paul had been distant and reserved, and that partly from native pride and partly from involuntary shrewdness she had treated the Comte de Manerville as in some sense her inferior and as though it were an honor for him to be allowed to marry Mademoiselle Evangelista. She assured Solonet that neither she nor her daughter could be suspected of any mercenary interests in the marriage; that they had the right, should Paul make any financial difficulties, to retreat from the affair to an illimitable distance; and finally, that she had already acquired over her future son-in-law a very remarkable ascendancy.

"If that is so," said Solonet, "tell me what are the utmost concessions you are willing to make."

"I wish to make as few as possible," she answered, laughing.

"A woman's answer," cried Solonet. "Madame, are you anxious to marry Mademoiselle Natalie?"

"Yes."

"And you want a receipt for the eleven hundred and fifty-six thousand francs, for which you are responsible on the guardianship account which the law obliges you to render to your son-in-law?"

"Yes."

"How much do you want to keep back?"

"Thirty thousand a year, at least."

"It is a question of conquer or die, is it?"

"It is."

"Well, then, I must reflect on the necessary means to that end; it will need all our cleverness to manage our forces. I will give you some instructions on my arrival this evening; follow them carefully, and I think I may promise you a successful issue. Is the Comte de Manerville in love with Mademoiselle Natalie?" he asked as he rose to take leave.

"He adores her."

"That is not enough. Does he desire her to the point of disregarding all pecuniary difficulties?"

"Yes."

"That's what I call having a lien upon a daughter's property," cried the notary. "Make her look her best to-night," he added with a sly glance.

"She has a most charming dress for the occasion."

"The marriage-contract dress is, in my opinion, half the battle," said Solonet.

This last argument seemed so cogent to Madame Evangelista that she superintended Natalie's toilet herself, as much perhaps to watch her daughter as to make her the innocent accomplice of her financial conspiracy.

With her hair dressed a la Sevigne and wearing a gown of white tulle adorned with pink ribbons, Natalie seemed to her mother so beautiful as to guarantee victory. When the lady's-maid left the room and Madame Evangelista was certain that no one could overhear her, she arranged a few curls on her daughter's head by way of exordium.

"Dear child," she said, in a voice that was firm apparently, "do you sincerely love the Comte de Manerville?"

Mother and daughter cast strange looks at each other.

"Why do you ask that question, little mother? and to-day more than yesterday> Why have you thrown me with him?"

"If you and I had to part forever would you still persist

in the marriage?"

"I should give it up - and I should not die of grief."

"You do not love him, my dear," said the mother, kissing her daughter's forehead.

"But why, my dear mother, are you playing the Grand Inquisitor?"

"I wished to know if you desired the marriage without being madly in love with the husband."

"I love him."

"And you are right. He is a count; we will make him a peer of France between us; nevertheless, there are certain difficulties."

"Difficulties between persons who love each other? Oh, no. The heart of the Pink of Fashion is too firmly planted here," she said, with a pretty gesture, "to make the very slightest objection. I am sure of that."

"But suppose it were otherwise?" persisted Madame Evangelista.

"He would be profoundly and forever forgotten," replied Natalie.

"Good! You are a Casa-Reale. But suppose, though he madly loves you, suppose certain discussions and difficulties should arise, not of his own making, but which he must decide in your interests as well as in mine - hey, Natalie, what then? Without lowering your dignity, perhaps a little softness in your manner might decide him - a word, a tone, a mere nothing. Men are so made; they resist a serious argument, but they yield to a tender look."

"I understand! a little touch to make my Favori leap the barrier," said Natalie, making the gesture of striking a horse with her whip.

"My darling! I ask nothing that resembles seduction. You and I have sentiments of the old Castilian honor which will never permit us to pass certain limits. Count Paul shall know our situation."

"What situation?"

"You would not understand it. But I tell you now that if after seeing you in all your glory his look betrays the slightest hesitation, - and I shall watch him, - on that instant I shall break off the marriage; I will liquidate my property, leave Bordeaux, and go to Douai, to be near the Claes. Madame Claes is our relation through the Temnincks. Then I'll marry you to a peer of France, and take refuge in a convent myself, that I may give up to you my whole fortune."

"Mother, what am I to do to prevent such misfortunes?" cried Natalie.

"I have never seen you so beautiful as you are now," replied her mother. "Be a little coquettish, and all is well."

Madame Evangelista left Natalie to her thoughts, and went to arrange her own toilet in such a way that would bear comparison with that of her daughter. If Natalie ought to make herself attractive to Paul she ought, none the less, to inflame the ardor of her champion Solonet. The mother and daughter were therefore under arms when Paul arrived, bearing the bouquet which for the last few months he had daily offered to his love. All three conversed pleasantly while awaiting the arrival of the notaries.

This day brought to Paul the first skirmish of that long and wearisome warfare called marriage. It is therefore necessary to state the forces on both sides, the position of the belligerent bodies, and the ground on which they are about to manoeuvre.

To maintain a struggle, the importance of which had wholly escaped him, Paul's only auxiliary was the old notary, Mathias. Both were about to be confronted, unaware and defenceless, by a most unexpected circumstance; to be pressed by an enemy whose strategy was planned, and driven to decide on a course without having time to reflect upon it. Where is the man who would not have succumbed, even though assisted by Cujas and Barthole? How should he look for deceit and treachery where all seemed compliant and natural? What could old Mathias do alone against Madame Evangelista, against Solonet, against Natalie, especially when a client in love goes over to the enemy as soon as the rising conflict threatens his happiness? Already Paul was damaging his cause by making the customary lover's speeches, to which his passion gave excessive value in the ears of Madame Evangelista, whose object it was to drive him to commit himself.

The matrimonial condottieri now about to fight for their clients, whose personal powers were to be so vitally important in this solemn encounter, the two notaries, on short, represent individually the old and the new systems, - old fashioned notarial usage, and the new-fangled modern procedure.

Maitre Mathias was a worthy old gentleman sixty-nine years of age, who took great pride in his forty years' exercise of the profession. His huge gouty feet were encased in shoes with silver buckles, making a ridiculous termination to legs so spindling, with knees so bony, that when he crossed them they made you think of the emblems on a tombstone. His puny little thighs, lost in a pair of wide black breeches fastened with buckles, seemed to bend beneath the weight of a round stomach and a torso developed, like that of most sedentary persons, into a stout barrel, always buttoned into a green coat with square tails, which no man could remember to have ever seen new. His hair, well brushed and powdered, was tied in a rat's tail that lay between the collar of his coat and that of his waistcoat, which was white, with a pattern of flowers. With his round head, his face the color of a vine-leaf, his blue eyes, a trumpet nose, a thick-lipped mouth, and a double-chin, the dear old fellow excited, whenever he appeared among strangers who did not know him, that satirical laugh which Frenchmen so generously bestow on the ludicrous creations Dame Nature occasionally allows herself, which Art delights in exaggerating under the name of caricatures.

But in Maitre Mathias, mind had triumphed over form; the qualities of his soul had vanquished the oddities of his body. The inhabitants of Bordeaux, as a rule, testified a friendly respect and a deference that was full of esteem for him. The old man's voice went to their hearts and sounded there with the eloquence of uprightness. His craft consisted in going straight to the fact, overturning all subterfuge and evil devices by plain questionings. His quick perception, his long training in his profession gave him that divining sense which goes to the depths of conscience and reads its secret thoughts. Though grave and deliberate in business, the patriarch could be gay with the gaiety of our ancestors. He could risk a song after dinner, enjoy all family festivities, celebrate the birthdays of grandmothers and children, and bury with due solemnity the Christmas log. He loved to send presents at New Year, and eggs at Easter; he believed in the duties of a godfather, and never deserted the customs which colored the life of the olden time. Maitre Mathias was a noble and venerable relic of the notaries, obscure great men, who gave no receipt for the millions entrusted to them, but returned those millions in the sacks they were delivered in, tied with the same twine; men who fulfilled their trusts to the letter, drew honest inventories, took fatherly interest in their clients, often barring the way to extravagance and dissipation, - men to whom families confided their secrets, and who felt so responsible for any error in their deeds that they meditated long and carefully over them. Never during his whole notarial life, had any client found reason to complain of a bad investment or an ill-placed mortgage. His own fortune, slowly but honorably acquired, had come to him as the result of a thirty years' practice and careful economy. He had established in life fourteen of his clerks. Religious, and generous in secret, Mathias was found whenever good was to be done without remuneration. An active member on hospital and other benevolent committees, he subscribed the largest sums to relieve all sudden misfortunes and emergencies, as well as to create certain useful permanent institutions; consequently, neither he nor his wife kept a carriage. Also his word was felt to be sacred, and his coffers held as much of the money of others as a bank; and also, we may add, he went by the name of "Our good Monsieur Mathias," and when he died, three thousand persons followed him to his grave.

Solonet was the style of young notary who comes in humming a tune, affects light-heartedness, declares that business is better done with a laugh than seriously. He is the notary captain of the national guard, who dislikes to be taken for a notary, solicits the cross of the Legion of honor, keeps his cabriolet, and leaves the verification of his deeds to his clerks; he is the notary who goes to balls and theatres, buys pictures and plays at ecarte; he has coffers in which gold is received on deposit and is later returned in bank-bills, - a notary who follows his epoch, risks capital in doubtful investments, speculates with all he can lay his hands on, and expects to retire with an income of thirty thousand francs after ten years' practice; in short, the notary whose cleverness comes of his duplicity, whom many men fear as an accomplice possessing their secrets, and who sees in his practice a means of ultimately marrying some blue-stockinged heiress.

When the slender, fair-haired Solonet, curled, perfumed, and booted like the leading gentleman at the Vaudeville, and dressed like a dandy whose most important business is a duel, entered Madame Evangelista's salon, preceding his brother notary, whose advance was delayed by a twinge of the gout, the two men presented to the life one of those famous caricatures entitled "Former Times and the Present Day," which had such eminent success under the Empire. If Madame and Mademoiselle Evangelista to whom the "good Monsieur Mathias," was personally unknown, felt, on first seeing him, a slight inclination to laugh, they were soon touched by the old-fashioned grace with which he greeted them. The words he used were full of that amenity which amiable old men convey as much by the ideas they suggest as by the manner in which they express them. The younger notary, with his flippant tone, seemed on a lower plane. Mathias showed his superior knowledge of life by the reserved manner with which he accosted Paul. Without compromising his white hairs, he showed that he respected the young man's nobility, while at the same time he claimed the honor due to old age, and made it felt that social rights are natural. Solonet's bow and greeting, on the contrary, expressed a sense of perfect equality, which would naturally affront the pretensions of a man of society and make the notary ridiculous in the eyes of a real noble. Solonet made a motion, somewhat too familiar, to Madame Evangelista, inviting her to a private conference in the recess of a window. For some minutes they talked to each other in a low voice, giving way now and then to laughter, - no doubt to lessen in the minds of others the importance of the conversation, in which Solonet was really communicating to his sovereign lady the plan of battle.

"But," he said, as he ended, "will you have the courage to sell your house?"

"Undoubtedly," she replied.

Madame Evangelista did not choose to tell her notary the motive of this heroism, which struck him greatly. Solonet's zeal might have cooled had he known that his client was really intending to leave Bordeaux. She had not as yet said anything about that intention to Paul, in order not to alarm him with the preliminary steps and circumlocutions which must be taken before he entered on the political life she planned for him.

After dinner the two plenipotentiaries left the loving pair with the mother, and betook themselves to an adjoining salon where their conference was arranged to take place. A dual scene then followed on this domestic stage: in the chimney-corner of the great salon a sceneof love, in which to all appearances life was smiles and joy; in the other room, a scene of gravity and gloom, where selfish interests, baldly proclaimed, openly took the part they play in life under flowery disguises.

"My dear master," said Solonet, "the document can remain under your lock and key; I know very well what I owe to my old preceptor." Mathias bowed gravely. "But," continued Solonet, unfolding the rough copy of a deed he had made his clerk draw up, "as we are the oppressed party, I mean the daughter, I have written the contract - which will save you trouble. We marry with our rights under the rule of community of interests; with general donation of our property to each other in case of death without heirs; if not, donation of one-fourth as life interest, and one-fourth in fee; the sum placed in community of interests to be one-fourth of the respective property of each party; the survivor to possess the furniture without appraisal. It's all as simple as how d'ye do."

"Ta, ta, ta, ta," said Mathias, "I don't do business as one sings a tune. What are your claims?"

"What are yours?" said Solonet.

"Our property," replied Mathias, "is: the estate of

Lanstrac, which brings in a rental of twenty-three thousand francs a year, not counting the natural products. Item: the farms of Grassol and Guadet, each worth three thousand six hundred francs a year. Item: the vineyard of Belle-Rose, yielding in ordinary years sixteen thousand francs; total, forty-six thousand two hundred francs a year. Item: the patrimonial mansion at Bordeaux taxed for nine hundred francs. Item: a handsome house, between court and garden in Paris, rue de la Pepiniere, taxed for fifteen hundred francs. These pieces of property, the title-deeds of which I hold, are derived from our father and mother, except the house in Paris, which we bought ourselves. We must also reckon in the furniture of the two houses, and that of the chateau of Lanstrac, estimated at four hundred and fifty thousand francs. There's the table, the cloth, and the first course. What do you bring for the second course and the dessert?"

"Our rights," replied Solonet.

"Specify them, my friend," said Mathias. "What do you bring us? Where is the inventory of the property left by Monsieur Evangelista? Show me the liquidation, the investment of the amount. Where is your capital? - if there is any capital. Where is your landed property? - if you have any. In short, let us see your guardianship account, and tell us what you bring and what your mother will secure to us."

"Does Monsieur le Comte de Manerville love Mademoiselle Evangelista?"

"He wishes to make her his wife if the marriage can be suitably arranged," said the old notary. "I am not a child; this matter concerns our business, and not our feelings."

"The marriage will be off unless you show generous feeling; and for this reason," continued Solonet. "No inventory was made at the death of our husband; we are Spaniards, Creoles, and know nothing of French laws. Besides, we were too deeply grieved at our loss to think at such a time of the miserable formalities which occupy cold hearts. It is publicly well known that our late husband adored us, and that we mourned for him sincerely. If we did have a settlement of accounts with a short inventory attached, made, as one may say, by common report, you can thank our surrogate guardian, who obliged us to establish a status and assign to our daughter a fortune, such as it is, at a time when we were forced to withdraw from London our English securities, the capital of which was immense, and re-invest the proceeds in Paris, where interests were doubled."

"Don't talk nonsense to me. There are various ways of verifying the property. What was the amount of your legacy tax? Those figures will enable us to get at the total. Come to the point. Tell us frankly what you received from the father's estate and how much remains of it. If we are very much in love we'll see then what we can do."

"If you are marrying us for our money you can go about your business. We have claims to more than a million; but all that remains to our mother is this house and furniture and four hundred odd thousand francs invested about 1817 in the Five-per-cents, which yield about forty-thousand francs a year."

"Then why do you live in a style that requires one

hundred thousand a year at the least?" cried Mathias, horror-stricken.

"Our daughter has cost us the eyes out of our head," replied Solonet. "Besides, we like to spend money. Your jeremiads, let me tell you, won't recover two farthings of the money."

"With the fifty thousand francs a year which belong to Mademoiselle Natalie you could have brought her up handsomely without coming to ruin. But if you have squandered everything while you were a girl what will it be when you are a married woman?"

"Then drop us altogether," said Solonet. "The handsomest girl in Bordeaux has a right to spend more than she has, if she likes."

"I'll talk to my client about that," said the old notary.

"Very good, old father Cassandra, go and tell your client that we haven't a penny," thought Solonet, who, in the solitude of his study, had strategically massed his forces, drawn up his propositions, manned the drawbridge of discussion, and prepared the point at which the opposing party, thinking the affair a failure, could suddenly be led into a compromise which would end in the triumph of his client.

The white dress with its rose-colored ribbons, the Sevigne curls, Natalie's tiny foot, her winning glance, her pretty fingers constantly employed in adjusting curls that needed no adjustment, these girlish manoeuvres like those of a peacock spreading his tail, had brought Paul to the point at which his future mother-in-law desired to see him. He was intoxicated with love, and his eyes, the sure thermometer of the soul, indicated the degree of passion at which a man commits a thousand follies.

"Natalie is so beautiful," he whispered to the mother, "that I can conceive the frenzy which leads a man to pay for his happiness by death."

Madame Evangelista replied with a shake of her head: -

"Lover's talk, my dear count. My husband never said such charming things to me; but he married me without a fortune and for thirteen years he never caused me one moment's pain."

"Is that a lesson you are giving me?" said Paul, laughing.

"You know how I love you, my dear son," she answered, pressing his hand. "I must indeed love you well to give you my Natalie."

"Give me, give me?" said the young girl, waving a screen of Indian feathers, "what are you whispering about me?"

"I was telling her," replied Paul, "how much I love you, since etiquette forbids me to tell it to you."

"Why?"

"I fear to say too much."

"Ah! you know too well how to offer the jewels of flattery. Shall I tell you my private opinion about you?

Well, I think you have more mind than a lover ought to have. To be the Pink of Fashion and a wit as well," she added, dropping her eyes, "is to have too many advantages: a man should choose between them. I fear too, myself."

"And why?"

"We must not talk in this way. Mamma, do you not think that this conversation is dangerous inasmuch as the contract is not yet signed?"

"It soon will be," said Paul.

"I should like to know what Achilles and Nestor are saying to each other in the next room," said Natalie, nodding toward the door of the little salon with a childlike expression of curiosity.

"They are talking of our children and our death and a lot of other such trifles; they are counting our gold to see if we can keep five horses in the stables. They are talking also of deeds of gift; but there, I have forestalled them."

"How so?"

"Have I not given myself wholly to you?" he said, looking straight at the girl, whose beauty was enhanced by the blush which the pleasure of this answer brought to her face.

"Mamma, how can I acknowledge so much generosity."

"My dear child, you have a lifetime before you in

which to return it. To make the daily happiness of a home, is to bring a treasure into it. I had no other fortune when I married."

"Do you like Lanstrac?" asked Paul, addressing Natalie.

"How could I fail to like the place where you were born?" she answered. "I wish I could see your house."

"*Our* house," said Paul. "Do you not want to know if I shall understand your tastes and arrange the house to suit you? Your mother had made a husband's task most difficult; you have always been so happy! But where love is infinite, nothing is impossible."

"My dear children," said Madame Evangelista, "do you feel willing to stay in Bordeaux after your marriage? If you have the courage to face the people here who know you and will watch and hamper you, so be it! But if you feel that desire for a solitude together which can hardly be expressed, let us go to Paris were the life of a young couple can pass unnoticed in the stream. There alone you can behave as lovers without fearing to seem ridiculous."

"You are quite right," said Paul, "but I shall hardly have time to get my house ready. However, I will write to-night to de Marsay, the friend on whom I can always count to get things done for me."

At the moment when Paul, like all young men accustomed to satisfy their desires without previous calculation, was inconsiderately binding himself to the expenses of a stay in Paris, Maitre Mathias entered the salon and made a sign to his client that he wished to speak to him.

"What is it, my friend?" asked Paul, following the old man to the recess of a window.

"Monsieur le comte," said the honest lawyer, "there is not a penny of dowry. My advice is: put off the conference to another day, so that you may gain time to consider your proper course."

"Monsieur Paul," said Natalie, "I have a word to say in private to you."

Though Madame Evangelista's face was calm, no Jew of the middle ages ever suffered greater torture in his caldron of boiling oil than she was enduring in her violet velvet gown. Solonet had pledged the marriage to her, but she was ignorant of the means and conditions of success. The anguish of this uncertainty was intolerable. Possibly she owed her safety to her daughter's disobedience. Natalie had considered the advice of her mother and noted her anxiety. When she saw the success of her own coquetry she was struck to the heart with a variety of contradictory thoughts. Without blaming her mother, she was half-ashamed of manoeuvres the object of which was, undoubtedly, some personal game. She was also seized with a jealous curiosity which is easily conceived. She wanted to find out if Paul loved her well enough to rise above the obstacles that her mother foresaw and which she now saw clouding the face of the old lawyer. These ideas and sentiments prompted her to an action of loyalty which became her well. But, for all that, the blackest perfidy could not have been as dangerous as her present innocence.

"Paul," she said in a low voice, and she so called him for the first time, "if any difficulties as to property arise to separate us, remember that I free you from all engagements, and will allow you to let the blame of such a rupture rest on me."

She put such dignity into this expression of her generosity that Paul believed in her disinterestedness and in her ignorance of the strange fact that his notary had just told to him. He pressed the young girl's hand and kissed it like a man to whom love is more precious than wealth. Natalie left the room.

"Sac-a-papier! Monsieur le comte, you are committing a great folly," said the old notary, rejoining his client.

Paul grew thoughtful. He had expected to unite Natalie's fortune with his own and thus obtain for his married life an income of one hundred thousand francs a year; and however much a man may be in love he cannot pass without emotion and anxiety from the prospect of a hundred thousand to the certainty of forty-six thousand a year and the duty of providing for a woman accustomed to every luxury.

"My daughter is no longer here," said Madame Evangelista, advancing almost regally toward her son-in-law and his notary. "May I be told what is happening?"

"Madame," replied Mathias, alarmed at Paul's silence, "an obstacle which I fear will delay us has arisen - "

At these words, Maitre Solonet issued from the little salon and cut short the old man's speech by a remark which restored Paul's composure. Overcome by the remembrance of his gallant speeches and his lover-like behavior, he felt unable to disown them or to change his course. He longed, for the moment, to fling himself into a gulf; Solonet's words relieved him.

"There is a way," said the younger notary, with an easy air, "by which madame can meet the payment which is due to her daughter. Madame Evangelista possesses forty thousand francs a year from an investment in the Five-per-cents, the capital of which will soon be at par, if not above it. We may therefore reckon it at eight hundred thousand francs. This house and garden are fully worth two hundred thousand. On that estimate, Madame can convey by the marriage contract the titles of that property to her daughter, reserving only a life interest in it - for I conclude that Monsieur le comte could hardly wish to leave his mother-in-law without means? Though Madame has certainly run through her fortune, she is still able to make good that of her daughter, or very nearly so."

"Women are most unfortunate in having no knowledge of business," said Madame Evangelista. "Have I titles to property? and what are life-interests?"

Paul was in a sort of ecstasy as he listened to this proposed arrangement. The old notary, seeing the trap, and his client with one foot caught in it, was petrified for a moment, as he said to himself: -

"I am certain they are tricking us."

"If madame will follow my advice," said Solonet, "she will secure her own tranquillity. By sacrificing herself in this way she may be sure that no minors will ultimately harass her - for we never know who may live and who may die! Monsieur le comte will then give due acknowledgment in the marriage contract of having received the sum total of Mademoiselle Evangelista's patrimonial inheritance."

Mathias could not restrain the indignation which shone in his eyes and flushed his face.

"And that sum," he said, shaking, "is - "

"One million, one hundred and fifty-six thousand francs according to the document - "

"Why don't you ask Monsieur le comte to make over 'hic et nunc' his whole fortune to his future wife?" said Mathias. "It would be more honest than what you now propose. I will not allow the ruin of the Comte de Manerville to take place under my very eyes - "

He made a step as if to address his client, who was silent throughout this scene as if dazed by it; but he turned and said, addressing Madame Evangelista: -

"Do not suppose, madame, that I think you a party to these ideas of my brother notary. I consider you an honest woman and a lady who knows nothing of business."

"Thank you, brother notary," said Solonet.

"You know that there can be no offence between you and me," replied Mathias. "Madame," he added, "you ought to know the result of this proposed arrangement. You are still young and beautiful enough to marry again - Ah! madame," said the old man, noting her gesture, "who can answer for themselves on that point?"

"I did not suppose, monsieur," said Madame Evangelista, "that, after remaining a widow for the seven best years of my life, and refusing the most brilliant offers for my daughter's sake, I should be suspected of such a piece of folly as marrying again at thirty-nine years of age. If we were not talking business I should regard your suggestion as an impertinence."

"Would it not be more impertinent if I suggested that you could not marry again?"

"Can and will are separate terms," remarked Solonet, gallantly.

"Well," resumed Maitre Mathias, "we will say nothing of your marriage. You may, and we all desire it, live for forty-five years to come. Now, if you keep for yourself the life-interest in your daughter's patrimony, your children are laid on the shelf for the best years of their lives."

"What does that mean?" said the widow. "I don't understand being laid on a shelf."

Solonet, the man of elegance and good taste, began to laugh.

"I'll translate it for you," said Mathias. "If your children are wise they will think of the future. To think of the future means laying by half our income, provided we have only two children, to whom we are bound to give a fine education and a handsome dowry.

Your daughter and son-in-law will, therefore, be reduced to live on twenty thousand francs a year, though each has spent fifty thousand while still unmarried. But that is nothing. The law obliges my client to account, hereafter, to his children for the eleven hundred and fifty-six thousand francs of their mother's patrimony; yet he may not have received them if his wife should die and madame should survive her, which may very well happen. To sign such a contract is to fling one's self into the river, bound hand and foot. You wish to make your daughter happy, do you not? If she loves her husband, a fact which notaries never doubt, she will share his troubles. Madame, I see enough in this scheme to make her die of grief and anxiety; you are consigning her to poverty. Yes, madame, poverty; to persons accustomed to the use of one hundred thousand francs a year, twenty thousand is poverty. Moreover, if Monsieur le comte, out of love for his wife, were guilty of extravagance, she could ruin him by exercising her rights when misfortunes overtook him. I plead now for you, for them, for their children, for every one."

"The old fellow makes a lot of smoke with his cannon," thought Maitre Solonet, giving his client a look, which meant, "Keep on!"

"There is one way of combining all interests," replied Madame Evangelista, calmly. "I can reserve to myself only the necessary cost of living in a convent, and my children can have my property at once. I can renounce the world, if such anticipated death conduces to the welfare of my daughter."

"Madame," said the old notary, "let us take time to consider and weigh, deliberately, the course we had best pursue to conciliate all interests."

"Good heavens! monsieur," cried Madame Evangelista, who saw defeat in delay, "everything has already been considered and weighed. I was ignorant of what the process of marriage is in France; I am a Spaniard and a Creole. I did not know that in order to marry my daughter it was necessary to reckon up the days which God may still grant me; that my child would suffer because I live; that I do harm by living, and by having lived! When my husband married me I had nothing but my name and my person. My name alone was a fortune to him, which dwarfed his own. What wealth can equal that of a great name? My dowry was beauty, virtue, happiness, birth, education. Can money give those treasures? If Natalie's father could overhear this conversation, his generous soul would be wounded forever, and his happiness in paradise destroyed. I dissipated, foolishly, perhaps, a few of his millions without a quiver ever coming to his eyelids. Since his death, I have grown economical and orderly in comparison with the life he encouraged me to lead - Come, let us break this thing off! Monsieur de Manerville is so disappointed that I - "

No descriptive language can express the confusion and shock which the words, "break off," introduced into the conversation. It is enough to say that these four apparently well-bred persons all talked at once.

"In Spain people marry in the Spanish fashion, or as they please; but in France they marry according to French law, sensibly, and as best they can," said Mathias.

"Ah, madame," cried Paul, coming out of his

stupefaction, "you mistake my feelings."

"This is not a matter of feeling," said the old notary, trying to stop his client from concessions. "We are concerned now with the interests and welfare of three generations. Have *we* wasted the missing millions? We are simply endeavoring to solve difficulties of which we are wholly guiltless."

"Marry us, and don't haggle," said Solonet.

"Haggle! do you call it haggling to defend the interests of father and mother and children?" said Mathias.

"Yes," said Paul, continuing his remarks to Madame Evangelista, "I deplore the extravagance of my youth, which does not permit me to stop this discussion, as you deplore your ignorance of business and your involuntary wastefulness. God is my witness that I am not thinking, at this moment, of myself. A simple life at Lanstrac does not alarm me; but how can I ask Mademoiselle Natalie to renounce her tastes, her habits? Her very existence would be changed."

"Where did Evangelista get his millions?" said the widow.

"Monsieur Evangelista was in business," replied the old notary; "he played in the great game of commerce; he despatched ships and made enormous sums; we are simply a landowner, whose capital is invested, whose income is fixed."

"There is still a way to harmonize all interests," said Solonet, uttering this sentence in a high falsetto tone, which silenced the other three and drew their eyes and their attention upon himself.

This young man was not unlike a skilful coachman who holds the reins of four horses, and amuses himself by first exciting his animals and then subduing them. He had let loose these passions, and then, in turn, he calmed them, making Paul, whose life and happiness were in the balance, sweat in his harness, as well as his own client, who could not clearly see her way through this involved discussion.

"Madame Evangelista," he continued, after a slight pause, "can resign her investment in the Five-per-cents at once, and she can sell this house. I can get three hundred thousand francs for it by cutting the land into small lots. Out of that sum she can give you one hundred and fifty thousand francs. In this way she pays down nine hundred thousand of her daughter's patrimony, immediately. That, to be sure, is not all that she owes her daughter, but where will you find, in France, a better dowry?"

"Very good," said Maitre Mathias; "but what, then, becomes of madame?"

At this question, which appeared to imply consent, Solonet said, softly, to himself, "Well done, old fox! I've caught you!"

"Madame," he replied, aloud, "will keep the hundred and fifty thousand francs remaining from the sale of the house. This sum, added to the value of her furniture, can be invested in an annuity which will give her twenty thousand francs a year. Monsieur le comte can arrange to provide a residence for her under his roof. Lanstrac is a large house. You have also a house in Paris," he went on, addressing himself to Paul. "Madame can, therefore, live with you wherever you are. A widow with twenty thousand francs a year, and no household to maintain, is richer than madame was when she possessed her whole fortune. Madame Evangelista has only this one daughter; Monsieur le comte is without relations; it will be many years before your heirs attain their majority; no conflict of interests is, therefore, to be feared. A mother-in-law and a son-in-law placed in such relations will form a household of united interests. Madame Evangelista can make up for the remaining deficit by paying a certain sum for her support from her annuity, which will ease your way. We know that madame is too generous and too large-minded to be willing to be a burden on her children. In this way you can make one household, united and happy, and be able to spend, in your own right, one hundred thousand francs a year. Is not that sum sufficient, Monsieur le comte, to enjoy, in all countries, the luxuries of life, and to satisfy all your wants and caprices? Believe me, a young couple often feel the need of a third member of the household; and, I ask you, what third member could be so desirable as a good mother?"

"A little paradise!" exclaimed the old notary.

Shocked to see his client's joy at this proposal, Mathias sat down on an ottoman, his head in his hands, plunged in reflections that were evidently painful. He knew well the involved phraseology in which notaries and lawyers wrap up, intentionally, malicious schemes, and he was not the man to be taken in by it. He now began, furtively, to watch his brother notary and Madame Evangelista as they conversed with Paul, endeavoring to detect some clew to the deep-laid plot which was beginning to appear upon the surface.

"Monsieur," said Paul to Solonet, "I thank you for the pains you take to conciliate our interests. This arrangement will solve all difficulties far more happily than I expected - if," he added, turning to Madame Evangelista, "it is agreeable to you, madame; for I could not desire anything that did not equally please you."

"I?" she said; "all that makes the happiness of my children is joy to me. Do not consider me in any way."

"That would not be right," said Paul, eagerly. "If your future is not honorably provided for, Natalie and I would suffer more than you would suffer for yourself."

"Don't be uneasy, Monsieur le comte," interposed Solonet.

"Ah!" thought old Mathias, "they'll make him kiss the rod before they scourge him."

"You may feel quite satisfied," continued Solonet. "There are so many enterprises going on in Bordeaux at this moment that investments for annuities can be negotiated on very advantageous terms. After deducting from the proceeds of the house and furniture the hundred and fifty thousand francs we owe you, I think I can guarantee to madame that two hundred and fifty thousand will remain to her. I take upon myself to invest that sum in a first mortgage on property worth a million, and to obtain ten per cent for it, - twenty-five thousand francs a year. Consequently, we are marrying on nearly equal fortunes. In fact, against your forty-six thousand francs a year, Mademoiselle Natalie brings you forty thousand a year in the Five-per-cents, and one hundred and fifty thousand in a round sum, which gives, in all, forty-seven thousand francs a year."

"That is evident," said Paul.

As he ended his speech, Solonet had cast a sidelong glance at his client, intercepted by Mathias, which meant: "Bring up your reserves."

"But," exclaimed Madame Evangelista, in tones of joy that did not seem to be feigned, "I can give Natalie my diamonds; they are worth, at least, a hundred thousand francs."

"We can have them appraised," said the notary. "This will change the whole face of things. Madame can then keep the proceeds of her house, all but fifty thousand francs. Nothing will prevent Monsieur le comte from giving us a receipt in due form, as having received, in full, Mademoiselle Natalie's inheritance from her father; this will close, of course, the guardianship account. If madame, with Spanish generosity, robs herself in this way to fulfil her obligations, the least that her children can do is to give her a full receipt."

"Nothing could be more just than that," said Paul. "I am simply overwhelmed by these generous proposals."

"My daughter is another myself," said Madame Evangelista, softly.

Maitre Mathias detected a look of joy on her face when she saw that the difficulties were being removed: that joy, and the previous forgetfulness of the diamonds, which were now brought forward like fresh troops, confirmed his suspicions.

"The scene has been prepared between them as gamblers prepare the cards to ruin a pigeon," thought the old notary. "Is this poor boy, whom I saw born, doomed to be plucked alive by that woman, roasted by his very love, and devoured by his wife? I, who have nursed these fine estates for years with such care, am I to see them ruined in a single night? Three million and a half to be hypothecated for eleven hundred thousand francs these women will force him to squander!"

Discovering thus in the soul of the elder woman intentions which, without involving crime, theft, swindling, or any actually evil or blameworthy action, nevertheless belonged to all those criminalities in embryo, Maitre Mathias felt neither sorrow nor generous indignation. He was not the Misanthrope; he was an old notary, accustomed in his business to the shrewd calculations of worldly people, to those clever bits of treachery which do more fatal injury than open murder on the high-road committed by some poor devil, who is guillotined in consequence. To the upper classes of society these passages in life, these diplomatic meetings and discussions are like the necessary cesspools where the filth of life is thrown. Full of pity for his client, Mathias cast a foreseeing eye into the future and saw nothing good.

"We'll take the field with the same weapons," thought he, "and beat them."

At this moment, Paul, Solonet and Madame Evangelista, becoming embarrassed by the old man's silence, felt that the approval of that censor was necessary to carry out the transaction, and all three turned to him simultaneously.

"Well, my dear Monsieur Mathias, what do you think of it?" said Paul.

"This is what I think," said the conscientious and uncompromising notary. "You are not rich enough to commit such regal folly. The estate of Lanstrac, if estimated at three per cent on its rentals, represents, with its furniture, one million; the farms of Grassol and Guadet and your vineyard of Belle-Rose are worth another million; your two houses in Bordeaux and Paris, with their furniture, a third million. Against those three millions, yielding forty-seven thousand francs a year, Mademoiselle Natalie brings eight hundred thousand francs in the Five-per-cents, the diamonds (supposing them to be worth a hundred thousand francs, which is still problematical) and fifty thousand francs in money; in all, one million and fifty thousand francs. In presence of such facts my brother notary tells you boastfully that we are marrying equal fortunes! He expects us to encumber ourselves with a debt of eleven hundred and fifty-six thousand francs to our children by acknowledging the receipt of our wife's patrimony, when we have actually received but little more than a doubtful million. You are listening to such stuff with the rapture of a lover, and you think that old Mathias, who is not in love, can forget arithmetic, and will not point out the difference between landed estate, the actual value of which is enormous and constantly increasing, and the revenues of personal property, the capital of which is subject to fluctuations and diminishment of income. I am old enough to have learned that money dwindles and land augments. You have called me in, Monsieur le comte, to stipulate for your interests; either let me defend those interests, or dismiss me."

"If monsieur is seeking a fortune equal in capital to his own," said Solonet, "we certainly cannot give it to him. We do not possess three millions and a half; nothing can be more evident. While you can boast of your three overwhelming millions, we can only produce our poor one million, - a mere nothing in your eyes, though three times the dowry of an archduchess of Austria. Bonaparte received only two hundred and fifty thousand francs with Maria-Louisa."

"Maria-Louisa was the ruin of Bonaparte," muttered Mathias.

Natalie's mother caught the words.

"If my sacrifices are worth nothing," she cried, "I do not choose to continue such a discussion; I trust to the discretion of Monsieur le comte, and I renounce the honor of his hand for my daughter."

According to the strategy marked out by the younger notary, this battle of contending interests had now reached the point where victory was certain for Madame Evangelista. The mother-in-law had opened her heart, delivered up her property, and was therefore practically released as her daughter's guardian. The future husband, under pain of ignoring the laws of generous propriety and being false to love, ought now to accept these conditions previously planned, and cleverly led up to by Solonet and Madame Evangelista. Like the hands of a clock turned by mechanism, Paul came faithfully up to time.

"Madame!" he exclaimed, "is it possible you can think of breaking off the marriage?"

"Monsieur," she replied, "to whom am I accountable? To my daughter. When she is twenty-one years of age she will receive my guardianship account and release me. She will then possess a million, and can, if she likes, choose her husband among the sons of the peers of France. She is a daughter of the Casa-Reale."

"Madame is right," remarked Solonet. "Why should she be more hardly pushed to-day than she will be fourteen months hence? You ought not to deprive her of the benefits of her maternity."

"Mathias," cried Paul, in deep distress, "there are two sorts of ruin, and you are bringing one upon me at this moment."

He made a step towards the old notary, no doubt intending to tell him that the contract must be drawn at once. But Mathias stopped that disaster with a glance which said, distinctly, "Wait!" He saw the tears in Paul's eyes, - tears drawn from an honorable man by the shame of this discussion as much as by the peremptory speech of Madame Evangelista, threatening rupture, - and the old man stanched them with a gesture like that of Archimedes when he cried, "Eureka!" The words "peer of France" had been to him like a torch in a dark crypt.

Natalie appeared at this moment, dazzling as the dawn, saying, with infantine look and manner, "Am I in the way?"

"Singularly so, my child," answered her mother, in a bitter tone.

"Come in, dear Natalie," said Paul, taking her hand and

leading her to a chair near the fireplace. "All is settled."

He felt it impossible to endure the overthrow of their mutual hopes.

"Yes, all can be settled," said Mathias, hastily interposing.

Like a general who, in a moment, upsets the plans skilfully laid and prepared by the enemy, the old notary, enlightened by that genius which presides over notaries, saw an idea, capable of saving the future of Paul and his children, unfolding itself in legal form before his eyes.

Maitre Solonet, who perceived no other way out of these irreconcilable difficulties than the resolution with which Paul's love inspired him, and to which this conflict of feelings and thwarted interests had brought him, was extremely surprised at the sudden exclamation of his brother notary. Curious to know the remedy that Mathias had found in a state of things which had seemed to him beyond all other relief, he said, addressing the old man: -

"What is it you propose?"

"Natalie, my dear child, leave us," said Madame Evangelista.

"Mademoiselle is not in the way," replied Mathias, smiling. "I am going to speak in her interests as well as in those of Monsieur le comte."

Silence reigned for a moment, during which time

everybody present, oppressed with anxiety, awaited the allocution of the venerable notary with unspeakable curiosity.

"In these days," continued Maitre Mathias, after a pause, "the profession of notary has changed from what it was. Political revolutions now exert an influence over the prospects of families, which never happened in former times. In those days existences were clearly defined; so were rank and position - "

"We are not here for a lecture on political ceremony, but to draw up a marriage contract," said Solonet, interrupting the old man, impatiently.

"I beg you to allow me to speak in my turn as I see fit," replied the other.

Solonet turned away and sat down on the ottoman, saying, in a low voice, to Madame Evangelista: -

"You will now hear what we call in the profession 'balderdash.'"

"Notaries are therefore compelled to follow the course of political events, which are now intimately connected with private interests. Here is an example: formerly noble families owned fortunes that were never shaken, but which the laws, promulgated by the Revolution, destroyed, and the present system tends to reconstruct," resumed the old notary, yielding to the loquacity of the "tabellionaris boa-constrictor" (boa-notary). "Monsieur le comte by his name, his talents, and his fortune is called upon to sit some day in the elective Chamber. Perhaps his destiny will take him to the hereditary Chamber, for we know that he has talent and means enough to fulfil that expectation. Do you not agree with me, madame?" he added, turning to the widow.

"You anticipate my dearest hope," she replied. "Monsieur de Manerville must be a peer of France, or I shall die of mortification."

"Therefore all that leads to that end -" continued Mathias with a cordial gesture to the astute mother-in-law.

"- will promote my eager desire," she replied.

"Well, then," said Mathias, "is not this marriage the proper occasion on which to entail the estate and create the family? Such a course would, undoubtedly, militate in the mind of the present government in favor of the nomination of my client whenever a batch of appointments is sent in. Monsieur le comte can very well afford to devote the estate of Lanstrac (which is worth a million) to this purpose. I do not ask that mademoiselle should contribute an equal sum; that would not be just. But we can surely apply eight hundred thousand of her patrimony to this object. There are two domains adjoining Lanstrac now to be sold, which can be purchased for that sum, which will return in rentals four and a half per cent. The house in Paris should be included in the entail. The surplus of the two fortunes, if judiciously managed, will amply suffice for the fortunes of the younger children. If the contracting parties will agree to this arrangement, Monsieur ought certainly to accept your guardianship account with its deficiency. I consent to that."

"Questa coda non e di questo gatto (That tail doesn't

belong to that cat)," murmured Madame Evangelista, appealing to Solonet.

"There's a snake in the grass somewhere," answered Solonet, in a low voice, replying to the Italian proverb with a French one.

"Why do you make this fuss?" asked Paul, leading Mathias into the adjoining salon.

"To save you from being ruined," replied the old notary, in a whisper. "You are determined to marry a girl and her mother who have already squandered two millions in seven years; you are pledging yourself to a debt of eleven hundred thousand francs to your children, to whom you will have to account for the fortune you are acknowledging to have received with their mother. You risk having your own fortune squandered in five years, and to be left as naked as Saint-John himself, besides being a debtor to your wife and children for enormous sums. If you are determined to put your life in that boat, Monsieur le comte, of course you can do as you choose; but at least let me, your old friend, try to save the house of Manerville."

"How is this scheme going to save it?" asked Paul.

"Monsieur le comte, you are in love - "

"Yes."

"A lover is about as discreet as a cannon-ball; therefore, I shall not explain. If you repeated what I should say, your marriage would probably be broken off. I protect your love by my silence. Have you confidence in my devotion?"

"A fine question!"

"Well, then, believe me when I tell you that Madame Evangelista, her notary, and her daughter, are tricking us through thick and thin; they are more than clever. Tudieu! what a sly game!"

"Not Natalie," cried Paul.

"I sha'n't put my fingers between the bark and the tree," said the old man. "You want her, take her! But I wish you were well out of this marriage, if it could be done without the least wrong-doing on your part."

"Why do you wish it?"

"Because that girl will spend the mines of Peru. Besides, see how she rides a horse, - like the groom of a circus; she is half emancipated already. Such girls make bad wives."

Paul pressed the old man's hand, saying, with a confident air of self-conceit: -

"Don't be uneasy as to that! But now, at this moment, what am I to do?"

"Hold firm to my conditions. They will consent, for no one's apparent interest is injured. Madame Evangelista is very anxious to marry her daughter; I see that in her little game - Beware of her!"

Paul returned to the salon, where he found his future mother-in-law conversing in a low tone with Solonet. Natalie, kept outside of these mysterious conferences, was playing with a screen. Embarrassed by her position, she was thinking to herself: "How odd it is that they tell me nothing of my own affairs."

The younger notary had seized, in the main, the future effect of the new proposal, based, as it was, on the self-love of both parties, into which his client had fallen headlong. Now, while Mathias was more than a mere notary, Solonet was still a young man, and brought into his business the vanity of youth. It often happens that personal conceit makes a man forgetful of the interests of his client. In this case, Maitre Solonet, who would not suffer the widow to think that Nestor had vanquished Achilles, advised her to conclude the marriage on the terms proposed. Little he cared for the future working of the marriage contract; to him, the conditions of victory were: Madame Evangelista released from her obligations as guardian, her future secured, and Natalie married.

"Bordeaux shall know that you have ceded eleven hundred thousand francs to your daughter, and that you still have twenty-five thousand francs a year left," whispered Solonet to his client. "For my part, I did not expect to obtain such a fine result."

"But," she said, "explain to me why the creation of this entail should have calmed the storm at once."

"It relieves their distrust of you and your daughter. An entail is unchangeable; neither husband nor wife can touch that capital."

"Then this arrangement is positively insulting!"

"No; we call it simply precaution. The old fellow has caught you in a net. If you refuse to consent to the entail, he can reply: 'Then your object is to squander the fortune of my client, who, by the creation of this entail, is protected from all such injury as securely as if the marriage took place under the "regime dotal."'"

Solonet quieted his own scruples by reflecting: "After all, these stipulations will take effect only in the future, by which time Madame Evangelista will be dead and buried."

Madame Evangelista contented herself, for the present, with these explanations, having full confidence in Solonet. She was wholly ignorant of law; considering her daughter as good as married, she thought she had gained her end, and was filled with the joy of success. Thus, as Mathias had shrewdly calculated, neither Solonet nor Madame Evangelista understood as yet, to its full extent, this scheme which he had based on reasons that were undeniable.

"Well, Monsieur Mathias," said the widow, "all is for the best, is it not?"

"Madame, if you and Monsieur le comte consent to this arrangement you ought to exchange pledges. It is fully understood, I suppose," he continued, looking from one to the other, "that the marriage will only take place on condition of creating an entail upon the estate of Lanstrac and the house in the rue de la Pepiniere, together with eight hundred thousand francs in money brought by the future wife, the said sum to be invested in landed property? Pardon me the repetition, madame; but a positive and solemn engagement becomes absolutely necessary. The creation of an entail requires formalities, application to the chancellor, a royal ordinance, and we ought at once to conclude the purchase of the new estate in order that the property be included in the royal ordinance by virtue of which it becomes inalienable. In many families this would be reduced to writing, but on this occasion I think a simple consent would suffice. Do you consent?"

"Yes," replied Madame Evangelista.

"Yes," said Paul.

"And I?" asked Natalie, laughing.

"You are a minor, mademoiselle," replied Solonet; "don't complain of that."

It was then agreed that Maitre Mathias should draw up the contract, Maitre Solonet the guardianship account and release, and that both documents should be signed, as the law requires some days before the celebration of the marriage. After a few polite salutations the notaries withdrew.

"It rains, Mathias; shall I take you home?" said Solonet. "My cabriolet is here."

"My carriage is here too," said Paul, manifesting an intention to accompany the old man.

"I won't rob you of a moment's pleasure," said Mathias. "I accept my friend Solonet's offer."

"Well," said Achilles to Nestor, as the cabriolet rolled away, "you have been truly patriarchal to-night. The fact is, those young people would certainly have ruined themselves."

"I felt anxious about their future," replied Mathias, keeping silent as to the real motives of his proposition.

At this moment the two notaries were like a pair of actors arm in arm behind the stage on which they have played a scene of hatred and provocation.

"But," said Solonet, thinking of his rights as notary, "isn't it my place to buy that land you mentioned? The money is part of our dowry."

"How can you put property bought in the name of Mademoiselle Evangelista into the creation of an entail by the Comte de Manerville?" replied Mathias.

"We shall have to ask the chancellor about that," said Solonet.

"But I am the notary of the seller as well as of the buyer of that land," said Mathias. "Besides, Monsieur de Manerville can buy in his own name. At the time of payment we can make mention of the fact that the dowry funds are put into it."

"You've an answer for everything, old man," said Solonet, laughing. "You were really surpassing to-night; you beat us squarely."

"For an old fellow who didn't expect your batteries of grape-shot, I did pretty well, didn't I?"

"Ha! ha! ha!" laughed Solonet.

The odious struggle in which the material welfare of a family had been so perilously near destruction was to the two notaries nothing more than a matter of professional polemics.

"I haven't been forty years in harness for nothing," remarked Mathias. "Look here, Solonet," he added, "I'm a good fellow; you shall help in drawing the deeds for the sale of those lands."

"Thanks, my dear Mathias. I'll serve you in return on the very first occasion."

While the two notaries were peacefully returning homeward, with no other sensations than a little throaty warmth, Paul and Madamc Evangelista were left a prey to the nervous trepidation, the quivering of the flesh and brain which excitable natures pass through after a scene in which their interests and their feelings have been violently shaken. In Madame Evangelista these last mutterings of the storm were overshadowed by a terrible reflection, a lurid gleam which she wanted, at any cost, to dispel.

"Has Maitre Mathias destroyed in a few minutes the work I have been doing for six months?" she asked herself. "Was he withdrawing Paul from my influence by filling his mind with suspicion during their secret conference in the next room?"

She was standing absorbed in these thoughts before the fireplace, her elbow resting on the marble mantel-shelf. When the porte-cochere closed behind the carriage of the two notaries, she turned to her future son-in-law, impatient to solve her doubts.

"This has been the most terrible day of my life," cried Paul, overjoyed to see all difficulties vanish. "I know no one so downright in speech as that old Mathias.

May God hear him, and make me peer of France! Dear Natalie, I desire this for your sake more than for my own. You are my ambition; I live only in you."

Hearing this speech uttered in the accents of the heart, and noting, more especially, the limpid azure of Paul's eyes, whose glance betrayed no thought of double meaning, Madame Evangelista's satisfaction was complete. She regretted the sharp language with which she had spurred him, and in the joy of success she resolved to reassure him as to the future. Calming her countenance, and giving to her eyes that expression of tender friendship which made her so attractive, she smiled and answered: -

"I can say as much to you. Perhaps, dear Paul, my Spanish nature has led me farther than my heart desired. Be what you are, - kind as God himself, - and do not be angry with me for a few hasty words. Shake hands."

Paul was abashed; he fancied himself to blame, and he kissed Madame Evangelista.

"Dear Paul," she said with much emotion, "why could not those two sharks have settled this matter without dragging us into it, since it was so easy to settle?"

"In that case I should not have known how grand and generous you can be," replied Paul.

"Indeed she is, Paul," cried Natalie, pressing his hand.

"We have still a few little matters to settle, my dear son," said Madame Evangelista. "My daughter and I are above the foolish vanities to which so many persons cling. Natalie does not need my diamonds, but I am glad to give them to her."

"Ah! my dear mother, do you suppose that I will accept them?"

"Yes, my child; they are one of the conditions of the contract."

"I will not allow it; I will not marry at all," cried Natalie, vehemently. "Keep those jewels which my father took such pride in collecting for you. How could Monsieur Paul exact - "

"Hush, my dear," said her mother, whose eyes now filled with tears. "My ignorance of business compels me to a greater sacrifice than that."

"What sacrifice?"

"I must sell my house in order to pay the money that I owe to you."

"What money can you possibly owe to me?" she said; "to me, who owe you life! If my marriage costs you the slightest sacrifice, I will not marry."

"Child!"

"Dear Natalie, try to understand that neither I, nor your mother, nor you yourself, require these sacrifices, but our children."

"Suppose I do not marry at all?"

"Do you not love me?" said Paul, tenderly.

"Come, come, my silly child; do you imagine that a contract is like a house of cards which you can blow down at will? Dear little ignoramus, you don't know what trouble we have had to found an entail for the benefit of your eldest son. Don't cast us back into the discussions from which we have just escaped."

"Why do you wish to ruin my mother?" said Natalie, looking at Paul.

"Why are you so rich?" he replied, smiling.

"Don't quarrel, my children, you are not yet married," said Madame Evangelista. "Paul," she continued, "you are not to give either corbeille, or jewels, or trousseau. Natalie has everything in profusion. Lay by the money you would otherwise put into wedding presents. I know nothing more stupidly bourgeois and commonplace than to spend a hundred thousand francs on a corbeille, when five thousand a year given to a young woman saves her much anxiety and lasts her lifetime. Besides, the money for a corbeille is needed to decorate your house in Paris. We will return to Lanstrac in the spring; for Solonet is to settle my debts during the winter."

"All is for the best," cried Paul, at the summit of happiness.

"So I shall see Paris!" cried Natalie, in a tone that would justly have alarmed de Marsay.

"If we decide upon this plan," said Paul, "I'll write to de Marsay and get him to take a box for me at the Bouffons and also at the Italian opera."

"You are very kind; I should never have dared to ask for it," said Natalie. "Marriage is a very agreeable institution if it gives husbands a talent for divining the wishes of their wives."

"It is nothing else," replied Paul. "But see how late it is; I ought to go."

"Why leave so soon to-night?" said Madame Evangelista, employing those coaxing ways to which men are so sensitive.

Though all this passed on the best of terms, and according to the laws of the most exquisite politeness, the effect of the discussion of these contending interests had, nevertheless, cast between son and mother-in-law a seed of distrust and enmity which was liable to sprout under the first heat of anger, or the warmth of a feeling too harshly bruised. In most families the settlement of "dots" and the deeds of gift required by a marriage contract give rise to primitive emotions of hostility, caused by self-love, by the lesion of certain sentiments, by regret for the sacrifices made, and by the desire to diminish them. When difficulties arise there is always a victorious side and a vanquished one. The parents of the future pair try to conclude the matter, which is purely commercial in their eyes, to their own advantage; and this leads to the trickery, shrewdness, and deception of such negotiations. Generally the husband alone is initiated into the secret of these discussions, and the wife is kept, like Natalie, in ignorance of the stipulations which make her rich or poor.

As he left the house, Paul reflected that, thanks to the cleverness of his notary, his fortune was almost entirely secured from injury. If Madame Evangelista did not live apart from her daughter their united household would have an income of more than a hundred thousand francs to spend. All his expectations of a happy and comfortable life would be realized.

"My mother-in-law seems to me an excellent woman," he thought, still under the influence of the cajoling manner by which she had endeavored to disperse the clouds raised by the discussion. "Mathias is mistaken. These notaries are strange fellows; they envenom everything. The harm started from that little cock-sparrow Solonet, who wanted to play a clever game."

While Paul went to bed recapitulating the advantages he had won during the evening, Madame Evangelista was congratulating herself equally on her victory.

"Well, darling mother, are you satisfied?" said Natalie, following Madame Evangelista into her bedroom.

"Yes, love," replied the mother, "everything went well, according to my wishes; I feel a weight lifted from my shoulders which was crushing me. Paul is a most easy-going man. Dear fellow! yes, certainly, we must make his life prosperous. You will make him happy, and I will be responsible for his political success. The Spanish ambassador used to be a friend of mine, and I'll renew the relation - as I will with the rest of my old acquaintance. Oh! you'll see! we shall soon be in the very heart of Parisian life; all will be enjoyment for us. You shall have the pleasures, my dearest, and I the last occupation of existence, - the game of ambition! Don't be alarmed when you see me selling this house. Do you suppose we shall ever come back to live in Bordeaux? no. Lanstrac? yes. But we shall spend all our winters in Paris, where our real interests lie. Well, Natalie, tell me, was it very difficult to do what I asked of you?"

"My little mamma! every now and then I felt ashamed."

"Solonet advises me to put the proceeds of this house into an annuity," said Madame Evangelista, "but I shall do otherwise; I won't take a penny of my fortune from you."

"I saw you were all very angry," said Natalie. "How did the tempest calm down?"

"By an offer of my diamonds," replied Madame Evangelista. "Solonet was right. How ably he conducted the whole affair. Get out my jewel-case, Natalie. I have never seriously considered what my diamonds are worth. When I said a hundred thousand francs I talked nonsense. Madame de Gyas always declared that the necklace and ear-rings your father gave me on our marriage day were worth at least that sum. My poor husband was so lavish! Then my family diamond, the one Philip the Second gave to the Duke of Alba, and which my aunt bequeathed to me, the 'Discreto,' was, I think, appraised in former times at four thousand quadruples, - one of our Spanish gold coins."

Natalie laid out upon her mother's toilet-table the pearl necklace, the sets of jewels, the gold bracelets and precious stones of all description, with that inexpressible sensation enjoyed by certain women at the sight of such treasures, by which - so commentators on the Talmud say - the fallen angels seduce the daughters of men, having sought these flowers of celestial fire in the bowels of the earth.

"Certainly," said Madame Evangelista, "though I know nothing about jewels except how to accept and wear them, I think there must be a great deal of money in these. Then, if we make but one household, I can sell my plate, the weight of which, as mere silver, would bring thirty thousand francs. I remember when we brought it from Lima, the custom-house officers weighed and appraised it. Solonet is right, I'll send to-morrow to Elie Magus. The Jew shall estimate the value of these things. Perhaps I can avoid sinking any of my fortune in an annuity."

"What a beautiful pearl necklace!" said Natalie.

"He ought to give it to you, if he loves you," replied her mother; "and I think he might have all my other jewels reset and let you keep them. The diamonds are a part of your property in the contract. And now, good-night, my darling. After the fatigues of this day we both need rest."

The woman of luxury, the Creole, the great lady, incapable of analyzing the results of a contract which was not yet in force, went to sleep in the joy of seeing her daughter married to a man who was easy to manage, who would let them both be mistresses of his home, and whose fortune, united to theirs, would require no change in their way of living. Thus having settled her account with her daughter, whose patrimony was acknowledged in the contract, Madame Evangelista could feel at her ease.

"How foolish of me to worry as I did," she thought.

"But I wish the marriage were well over."

So Madame Evangelista, Paul, Natalie, and the two notaries were equally satisfied with the first day's result. The Te Deum was sung in both camps, - a dangerous situation; for there comes a moment when the vanquished side is aware of its mistake. To Madame Evangelista's mind, her son-in-law was the vanquished side.

CHAPTER IV

THE MARRIAGE CONTRACT - SECOND DAY

The next day Elie Magus (who happened at that time to be in Bordeaux) obeyed Madame Evangelista's summons, believing, from general rumor as to the marriage of Comte Paul with Mademoiselle Natalie, that it concerned a purchase of jewels for the bride. The Jew was, therefore, astonished when he learned that, on the contrary, he was sent for to estimate the value of the mother-in-law's property. The instinct of his race, as well as certain insidious questions, made him aware that the value of the diamonds was included in the marriage-contract. The stones were not to be sold, and yet he was to estimate them as if some private person were buying them from a dealer. Jewellers alone know how to distinguish between the diamonds of Asia and those of Brazil. The stones of Golconda and Visapur are known by a whiteness and glittering brilliancy which others have not, - the water of the Brazilian diamonds having a yellow tinge which reduces their selling value. Madame Evangelista's necklace and ear-rings, being composed entirely of Asiatic diamonds, were valued by Elie Magus at two hundred and fifty thousand francs. As for the "Discreto," he pronounced it one of the finest diamonds in the possession of private persons; it was known to the trade and valued at one hundred thousand francs. On hearing this estimate, which proved to her the lavishness of her husband, Madame Evangelista asked the old Jew whether she should be able to obtain that money immediately.

"Madame," replied the Jew, "if you wish to sell I can give you only seventy-five thousand for the brilliant, and one hundred and sixty thousand for the necklace and earrings."

"Why such reduction?"

"Madame," replied Magus, "the finer the diamond, the longer we keep it unsold. The rarity of such investments is one reason for the high value set upon precious stones. As the merchant cannot lose the interest of his money, this additional sum, joined to the rise and fall to which such merchandise is subject, explains the difference between the price of purchase and the price of sale. By owning these diamonds you have lost the interest on three hundred thousand francs for twenty years. If you wear your jewels ten times a year, it costs you three thousand francs each evening to put them on. How many beautiful gowns you could buy with that sum. Those who own diamonds are, therefore, very foolish; but, luckily for us, women are never willing to understand the calculation."

"I thank you for explaining it to me, and I shall profit by it."

"Do you wish to sell?" asked Magus, eagerly.

"What are the other jewels worth?"

The Jew examined the gold of the settings, held the

pearls to the light, scrutinized the rubies, the diadems, clasps, bracelets, and chains, and said, in a mumbling tone: -

"A good many Portuguese diamonds from Brazil are among them. They are not worth more than a hundred thousand to me. But," he added, "a dealer would sell them to a customer for one hundred and fifty thousand, at least."

"I shall keep them," said Madame Evangelista.

"You are wrong," replied Elie Magus. "With the income from the sum they represent you could buy just as fine diamonds in five years, and have the capital to boot."

This singular conference became known, and corroborated certain rumors excited by the discussion of the contract. The servants of the house, overhearing high voices, supposed the difficulties greater than they really were. Their gossip with other valets spread the information, which from the lower regions rose to the ears of the masters. The attention of society, and of the town in general, became so fixed on the marriage of two persons equally rich and well-born, that every one, great and small, busied themselves about the matter, and in less than a week the strangest rumors were bruited about.

"Madame Evangelista sells her house; she must be ruined. She offered her diamonds to Elie Magus. Nothing is really settled between herself and the Comte de Manerville. Is it probable that the marriage will ever take place?"

To this question some answered yes, and others said no. The two notaries, when questioned, denied these calumnies, and declared that the difficulties arose only from the official delay in constituting the entail. But when public opinion has taken a trend in one direction it is very difficult to turn it back. Though Paul went every day to Madame Evangelista's house, and though the notaries denied these assertions continually, the whispered calumny went on. Young girls, and their mothers and aunts, vexed at a marriage they had dreamed of for themselves or for their families, could not forgive the Spanish ladies for their happiness, as authors cannot forgive each other for their success. A few persons revenged themselves for the twenty-years luxury and grandeur of the family of Evangelista, which had lain heavily on their self-love. A leading personage at the prefecture declared that the notaries could have chosen no other language and followed no other conduct in the case of a rupture. The time actually required for the establishment of the entail confirmed the suspicions of the Bordeaux provincials.

"They will keep the ball going through the winter; then, in the spring, they will go to some watering-place, and we shall learn before the year is out that the marriage is off."

"And, of course, we shall be given to understand," said others, "for the sake of the honor of the two families, that the difficulties did not come from either side, but the chancellor refused to consent; you may be sure it will be some quibble about that entail which will cause the rupture."

"Madame Evangelista," some said, "lived in a style that the mines of Valencia couldn't meet. When the time came to melt the bell, and pay the daughter's patrimony, nothing would be found to pay it with."

The occasion was excellent to add up the spendings of the handsome widow and prove, categorically, her ruin. Rumors were so rife that bets were made for and against the marriage. By the laws of worldly jurisprudence this gossip was not allowed to reach the ears of the parties concerned. No one was enemy or friend enough to Paul or to Madame Evangelista to inform either of what was being said. Paul had some business at Lanstrac, and used the occasion to make a hunting-party for several of the young men of Bordeaux, - a sort of farewell, as it were, to his bachelor life. This hunting party was accepted by society as a signal confirmation of public suspicion.

When this event occurred, Madame de Gyas, who had a daughter to marry, thought it high time to sound the matter, and to condole, with joyful heart, the blow received by the Evangelistas. Natalie and her mother were somewhat surprised to see the lengthened face of the marquise, and they asked at once if anything distressing had happened to her.

"Can it be," she replied, "that you are ignorant of the rumors that are circulating? Though I think them false myself, I have come to learn the truth in order to stop this gossip, at any rate among the circle of my own friends. To be the dupes or the accomplices of such an error is too false a position for true friends to occupy."

"But what is it? what has happened?" asked mother and daughter.

Madame de Gyas thereupon allowed herself the

happiness of repeating all the current gossip, not sparing her two friends a single stab. Natalie and Madame Evangelista looked at each other and laughed, but they fully understood the meaning of the tale and the motives of their friend. The Spanish lady took her revenge very much as Celimene took hers on Arsinoe.

"My dear, are you ignorant - you who know the provinces so well - can you be ignorant of what a mother is capable when she has on her hands a daughter whom she cannot marry for want of 'dot' and lovers, want of beauty, want of mind, and, sometimes, want of everything? Why, a mother in that position would rob a diligence or commit a murder, or wait for a man at the corner of a street - she would sacrifice herself twenty times over, if she was a mother at all. Now, as you and I both know, there are many such in that situation in Bordeaux, and no doubt they attribute to us their own thoughts and actions. Naturalists have depicted the habits and customs of many ferocious animals, but they have forgotten the mother and daughter in quest of a husband. Such women are hyenas, going about, as the Psalmist says, seeking whom they may devour, and adding to the instinct of the brute the intellect of man, and the genius of woman. I can understand that those little spiders, Mademoiselle de Belor, Mademoiselle de Trans, and others, after working so long at their webs without catching a fly, without so much as hearing a buzz, should be furious; I can even forgive their spiteful speeches. But that you, who can marry your daughter when you please, you, who are rich and titled, you who have nothing of the provincial about you, whose daughter is clever and possesses fine qualities, with beauty and the power to choose - that you, so distinguished from the rest by your Parisian grace, should have paid the least heed to this talk does really surprise me. Am I bound to account to the public for the marriage stipulations which our notaries think necessary under the political circumstances of my son-in-law's future life? Has the mania for public discussion made its way into families? Ought I to convoke in writing the fathers and mothers of the province to come here and give their vote on the clauses of our marriage contract?"

A torrent of epigram flowed over Bordeaux. Madame Evangelista was about to leave the city, and could safely scan her friends and enemies, caricature them and lash them as she pleased, with nothing to fear in return. Accordingly, she now gave vent to her secret observations and her latent dislikes as she sought for the reason why this or that person denied the shining of the sun at mid-day.

"But, my dear," said the Marquise de Gyas, "this stay of the count at Lanstrac, these parties given to young men under such circumstances - "

"Ah! my dear," said the great lady, interrupting the marquise, "do you suppose that we adopt the pettiness of bourgeois customs? Is Count Paul held in bonds like a man who might seek to get away? Think you we ought to watch him with a squad of gendarmes lest some provincial conspiracy should get him away from us?"

"Be assured, my dearest friend, that it gives me the greatest pleasure to - "

Here her words were interrupted by a footman who entered the room to announce Paul. Like many lovers,

Paul thought it charming to ride twelve miles to spend an hour with Natalie. He had left his friends while hunting, and came in booted and spurred, and whip in hand.

"Dear Paul," said Natalie, "you don't know what an answer you are giving to madame."

When Paul heard of the gossip that was current in Bordeaux, he laughed instead of being angry.

"These worthy people have found out, perhaps, that there will be no wedding festivities, according to provincial usages, no marriage at mid-day in the church, and they are furious. Well, my dear mother," he added, kissing her hand, "let us pacify them with a ball on the day when we sign the contract, just as the government flings a fete to the people in the great square of the Champs-Elysees, and we will give our dear friends the dolorous pleasure of signing a marriage-contract such as they have seldom heard of in the provinces."

This little incident proved of great importance. Madame Evangelista invited all Bordeaux to witness the signature of the contract, and showed her intention of displaying in this last fete a luxury which should refute the foolish lies of the community.

The preparations for this event required over a month, and it was called the fete of the camellias. Immense quantities of that beautiful flower were massed on the staircase, and in the antechamber and supper-room. During this month the formalities for constituting the entail were concluded in Paris; the estates adjoining Lanstrac were purchased, the banns were published, and all doubts finally dissipated. Friends and enemies thought only of preparing their toilets for the coming fete.

The time occupied by these events obscured the difficulties raised by the first discussion, and swept into oblivion the words and arguments of that stormy conference. Neither Paul nor his mother-in-law continued to think of them. Were they not, after all, as Madame Evangelista had said, the affair of the two notaries?

But - to whom has it never happened, when life is in its fullest flow, to be suddenly changed by the voice of memory, raised, perhaps, too late, reminding us of some important new fact, some threatened danger? On the morning of the day when the contract was to be signed and the fete given, one of these flashes of the soul illuminated the mind of Madame Evangelista during the semi-somnolence of her waking hour. The words that she herself had uttered at the moment when Mathias acceded to Solonet's conditions, "Questa coda non e di questo gatto," were cried aloud in her mind by that voice of memory. In spite of her incapacity for business, Madame Evangelista's shrewdness told her: -

"If so clever a notary as Mathias was pacified, it must have been that he saw compensation at the cost of *some one*."

That some one could not be Paul, as she had blindly hoped. Could it be that her daughter's fortune was to pay the costs of war? She resolved to demand explanations on the tenor of the contract, not reflecting on the course she would have to take in case she found her interests seriously compromised. This day had so powerful an influence on Paul de Manerville's conjugal life that it is necessary to explain certain of the external circumstances which accompanied it.

Madame Evangelista had shrunk from no expense for this dazzling fete. The court-yard was gravelled and converted into a tent, and filled with shrubs, although it was winter. The camellias, of which so much had been said from Angouleme to Dax, were banked on the staircase and in the vestibules. Wall partitions had disappeared to enlarge the supper-room and the ball-room where the dancing was to be. Bordeaux, a city famous for the luxury of colonial fortunes, was on a tiptoe of expectation for this scene of fairyland. About eight o'clock, as the last discussion of the contract was taking place within the house, the inquisitive populace, anxious to see the ladies in full dress getting out of their carriages, formed in two hedges on either side of the porte-cochere. Thus the sumptuous atmosphere of a fete acted upon all minds at the moment when the contract was being signed, illuminating colored lamps lighted up the shrubs, and the wheels of the arriving guests echoed from the court-yard. The two notaries had dined with the bridal pair and their mother. Mathias's head-clerk, whose business it was to receive the signatures of the guests during the evening (taking due care that the contract was not surreptitiously read by the signers), was also present at the dinner.

No bridal toilet was ever comparable with that of Natalie, whose beauty, decked with laces and satin, her hair coquettishly falling in a myriad of curls about her throat, resembled that of a flower encased in its foliage. Madame Evangelista, robed in a gown of cherry velvet, a color judiciously chosen to heighten the brilliancy of her skin and her black hair and eyes, glowed with the beauty of a woman at forty, and wore her pearl necklace, clasped with the "Discreto," a visible contradiction to the late calumnies.

To fully explain this scene, it is necessary to say that Paul and Natalie sat together on a sofa beside the fireplace and paid no attention to the reading of the documents. Equally childish and equally happy, regarding life as a cloudless sky, rich, young, and loving, they chattered to each other in a low voice, sinking into whispers. Arming his love with the presence of legality, Paul took delight in kissing the tips of Natalie's fingers, in lightly touching her snowy shoulders and the waving curls of her hair, hiding from the eyes of others these joys of illegal emancipation. Natalie played with a screen of peacock's feathers given to her by Paul, - a gift which is to love, according to superstitious belief in certain countries, as dangerous an omen as the gift of scissors or other cutting instruments, which recall, no doubt, the Parces of antiquity.

Seated beside the two notaries, Madame Evangelista gave her closest attention to the reading of the documents. After listening to the guardianship account, most ably written out by Solonet, in which Natalie's share of the three million and more francs left by Monsieur Evangelista was shown to be the much-debated eleven hundred and fifty-six thousand, Madame Evangelista said to the heedless young couple: -

"Come, listen, listen, my children; this is your marriage contract."

The clerk drank a glass of iced-water, Solonet and

Mathias blew their noses, Paul and Natalie looked at the four personages before them, listened to the preamble, and returned to their chatter. The statement of the property brought by each party; the general deed of gift in the event of death without issue; the deed of gift of one-fourth in life-interest and one-fourth in capital without interest, allowed by the Code, whatever be the number of the children; the constitution of a common fund for husband and wife; the settlement of the diamonds on the wife, the library and horses on the husband, were duly read and passed without observations. Then followed the constitution of the entail. When all was read and nothing remained but to sign the contract, Madame Evangelista demanded to know what would be the ultimate effect of the entail.

"An entail, madam," replied Solonet, "means an inalienable right to the inheritance of certain property belonging to both husband and wife, which is settled from generation to generation on the eldest son of the house, without, however, depriving him of his right to share in the division of the rest of the property."

"What will be the effect of this on my daughter's rights?"

Maitre Mathias, incapable of disguising the truth, replied: -

"Madame, an entail being an appanage, or portion of property set aside for this purpose from the fortunes of husband and wife, it follows that if the wife dies first, leaving several children, one of them a son, Monsieur de Manerville will owe those children three hundred and sixty thousand francs only, from which he will deduct his fourth in life-interest and his fourth in capital. Thus his debt to those children will be reduced to one hundred and sixty thousand francs, or thereabouts, exclusive of his savings and profits from the common fund constituted for husband and wife. If, on the contrary, he dies first, leaving a male heir, Madame de Manerville has a right to three hundred and sixty thousand francs only, and to her deeds of gift of such of her husband's property as is not included in the entail, to the diamonds now settled upon her, and to her profits and savings from the common fund."

The effect of Maitre Mathias's astute and far-sighted policy were now plainly seen.

"My daughter is ruined," said Madame Evangelista in a low voice.

The old and the young notary both overheard the words.

"Is it ruin," replied Mathias, speaking gently, "to constitute for her family an indestructible fortune?"

The younger notary, seeing the expression of his client's face, thought it judicious in him to state the disaster in plain terms.

"We tried to trick them out of three hundred thousand francs," he whispered to the angry woman. "They have actually laid hold of eight hundred thousand; it is a loss of four hundred thousand from our interests for the benefit of the children. You must now either break the marriage off at once, or carry it through," concluded Solonet.

It is impossible to describe the moment of silence that

followed. Maitre Mathias waited in triumph the signature of the two persons who had expected to rob his client. Natalie, not competent to understand that she had lost half her fortune, and Paul, ignorant that the house of Manerville had gained it, were laughing and chattering still. Solonet and Madame Evangelista gazed at each other; the one endeavoring to conceal his indifference, the other repressing the rush of a crowd of bitter feelings.

After suffering in her own mind the struggles of remorse, after blaming Paul as the cause of her dishonesty, Madame Evangelista had decided to employ those shameful manoeuvres to cast on him the burden of her own unfaithful guardianship, considering him her victim. But now, in a moment, she perceived that where she thought she triumphed she was about to perish, and her victim was her own daughter. Guilty without profit, she saw herself the dupe of an honorable old man, whose respect she had doubtless lost. Her secret conduct must have inspired the stipulation of old Mathias; and Mathias must have enlightened Paul. Horrible reflection! Even if he had not yet done so, as soon as that contract was signed the old wolf would surely warn his client of the dangers he had run and had now escaped, were it only to receive the praise of his sagacity. He would put him on his guard against the wily woman who had lowered herself to this conspiracy; he would destroy the empire she had conquered over her son-in-law! Feeble natures, once warned, turn obstinate, and are never won again. At the first discussion of the contract she had reckoned on Paul's weakness, and on the impossibility he would feel of breaking off a marriage so far advanced. But now, she herself was far more tightly bound. Three months earlier Paul had no real obstacles to prevent the rupture; now, all Bordeaux knew that the notaries had smoothed the difficulties; the banns were published; the wedding was to take place immediately; the friends of both families were at that moment arriving for the fete, and to witness the contract. How could she postpone the marriage at this late hour? The cause of the rupture would surely be made known; Maitre Mathias's stern honor was too well known in Bordeaux; his word would be believed in preference to hers. The scoffers would turn against her and against her daughter. No, she could not break it off; she must yield!

These reflections, so cruelly sound, fell upon Madame Evangelista's brain like a water-spout and split it. Though she still maintained the dignity and reserve of a diplomatist, her chin was shaken by that apoplectic movement which showed the anger of Catherine the Second on the famous day when, seated on her throne and in presence of her court (very much in the present circumstances of Madame Evangelista), she was braved by the King of Sweden. Solonet observed that play of the muscles, which revealed the birth of a mortal hatred, a lurid storm to which there was no lightning. At this moment Madame Evangelista vowed to her son-in-law one of those unquenchable hatreds the seeds of which were left by the Moors in the atmosphere of Spain.

"Monsieur," she said, bending to the ear of her notary, "you called that stipulation balderdash; it seems to me that nothing could have been more clear."

"Madame, allow me - "

"Monsieur," she continued, paying no heed to his

interruption, "if you did not perceive the effect of that entail at the time of our first conference, it is very extraordinary that it did not occur to you in the silence of your study. This can hardly be incapacity."

The young notary drew his client into the next room, saying to himself, as he did so: -

"I get a three-thousand franc fee for the guardianship account, three thousand for the contract, six thousand on the sale of the house, fifteen thousand in all - better not be angry."

He closed the door, cast on Madame Evangelista the cool look of a business man, and said: -

"Madame, having, for your sake, passed - as I did - the proper limits of legal craft, do you seriously intend to reward my devotion by such language?"

"But, monsieur - "

"Madame, I did not, it is true, calculate the effect of the deeds of gift. But if you do not wish Comte Paul for your son-in-law you are not obliged to accept him. The contract is not signed. Give your fete, and postpone the signing. It is far better to brave Bordeaux than sacrifice yourself."

"How can I justify such a course to society, which is already prejudiced against us by the slow conclusion of the marriage?"

"By some error committed in Paris; some missing document not sent with the rest," replied Solonet.

"But those purchases of land near Lanstrac?"

"Monsieur de Manerville will be at no loss to find another bride and another dowry."

"Yes, he'll lose nothing; but we lose all, all!"

"You?" replied Solonet; "why, you can easily find another count who will cost you less money, if a title is the chief object of this marriage."

"No, no! we can't stake our honor in that way. I am caught in a trap, monsieur. All Bordeaux will ring with this to-morrow. Our solemn words are pledged - "

"You wish the happiness of Mademoiselle Natalie."

"Above all things."

"To be happy in France," said the notary, "means being mistress of the home. She can lead that fool of a Manerville by the nose if she chooses; he is so dull he has actually seen nothing of all this. Even if he now distrusts you, he will always trust his wife; and his wife is YOU, is she not? The count's fate is still within your power if you choose to play the cards in your hand."

"If that were true, monsieur, I know not what I would not do to show my gratitude," she said, in a transport of feeling that colored her cheeks.

"Let us now return to the others, madame," said Solonet. "Listen carefully to what I shall say; and then - you shall think me incapable if you choose."

"My dear friend," said the young notary to Maitre Mathias, "in spite of your great ability, you have not foreseen either the case of Monsieur de Manerville dying without children, nor that in which he leaves only female issue. In either of those cases the entail would pass to the Manervilles, or, at any rate, give rise to suits on their part. I think, therefore, it is necessary to stipulate that in the first case the entailed property shall pass under the general deed of gift between husband and wife; and in the second case that the entail shall be declared void. This agreement concerns the wife's interest."

"Both clauses seem to me perfectly just," said Maitre Mathias. "As to their ratification, Monsieur le comte can, doubtless, come to an understanding with the chancellor, if necessary."

Solonet took a pen and added this momentous clause on the margin of the contract. Paul and Natalie paid no attention to the matter; but Madame Evangelista dropped her eyes while Maitre Mathias read the added sentence aloud.

"We will now sign," said the mother.

The volume of voice which Madame Evangelista repressed as she uttered those words betrayed her violent emotion. She was thinking to herself: "No, my daughter shall not be ruined - but he! My daughter shall have the name, the title, and the fortune. If she should some day discover that she does not love him, that she loves another, irresistibly, Paul shall be driven out of France! My daughter shall be free, and happy, and rich."

If Maitre Mathias understood how to analyze business interests, he knew little of the analysis of human passions. He accepted Madame Evangelista's words as an honorable "amende," instead of judging them for what they were, a declaration of war. While Solonet and his clerk superintended Natalie as she signed the documents, - an operation which took time, - Mathias took Paul aside and told him the meaning of the stipulation by which he had saved him from ultimate pain.

"The whole affair is now 'en regle.' I hold the documents. But the contract contains a rescript for the diamonds; you must ask for them. Business is business. Diamonds are going up just now, but may go down. The purchase of those new domains justifies you in turning everything into money that you can. Therefore, Monsieur le comte, have no false modesty in this matter. The first payment is due after the formalities are over. The sum is two hundred thousand francs; put the diamonds into that. You have the lien on this house, which will be sold at once, and will pay the rest. If you have the courage to spend only fifty thousand francs for the next three years, you can save the two hundred thousand francs you are now obliged to pay. If you plant vineyards on your new estates, you can get an income of over twenty-five thousand francs upon them. You may be said, in short, to have made a good marriage."

Paul pressed the hand of his old friend very affectionately, a gesture which did not escape Madame Evangelista, who now came forward to offer him the pen. Suspicion became certainty to her mind. She was confident that Paul and Mathias had come to an understanding about her. Rage and hatred sent the blood surging through her veins to her heart. The worst had come.

After verifying that all the documents were duly signed and the initials of the parties affixed to the bottom of the leaves, Maitre Mathias looked from Paul to his mother-in-law, and seeing that his client did not intend to speak of the diamonds, he said: -

"I do not suppose there can be any doubt about the transfer of the diamonds, as you are now one family."

"It would be more regular if Madame Evangelista made them over now, as Monsieur de Manerville has become responsible for the guardianship funds, and we never know who may live or die," said Solonet, who thought he saw in this circumstance fresh cause of anger in the mother-in-law against the son-in-law.

"Ah! mother," cried Paul, "it would be insulting to us all to do that, - 'Summum jus, summum injuria,' monsieur," he said to Solonet.

"And I," said Madame Evangelista, led by the hatred now surging in her heart to see a direct insult to her in the indirect appeal of Maitre Mathias, "I will tear that contract up if you do not take them."

She left the room in one of those furious passions which long for the power to destroy everything, and which the sense of impotence drives almost to madness.

"For Heaven's sake, take them, Paul," whispered Natalie in his ear.

"My mother is angry; I shall know why to-night, and I will tell you. We must pacify her."

Calmed by this first outburst, madame kept the necklace and ear-rings, which she was wearing, and brought the other jewels, valued at one hundred and fifty thousand francs by Elie Magus. Accustomed to the sight of family diamonds in all valuations of inheritance, Maitre Mathias and Solonet examined these jewels in their cases and exclaimed upon their duty.

"You will lose nothing, after all, upon the 'dot,' Monsieur le comte," said Solonet, bringing the color to Paul's face.

"Yes," said Mathias, "these jewels will meet the first payment on the purchase of the new estate."

"And the costs of the contract," added Solonet.

Hatred feeds, like love, on little things; the least thing strengthens it; as one beloved can do no evil, so the person hated can do no good. Madame Evangelista assigned to hypocrisy the natural embarrassment of Paul, who was unwilling to take the jewels, and not knowing where to put the cases, longed to fling them from the window. Madame Evangelista spurred him with a glance which seemed to say, "Take your property from here."

"Dear Natalie," said Paul, "put away these jewels; they are yours; I give them to you."

Natalie locked them into the drawer of a console. At this instant the noise of the carriages in the court-yard and the murmur of voices in the receptions-rooms became so loud that Natalie and her mother were forced to appear. The salons were filled in a few moments, and the fete began.

"Profit by the honeymoon to sell those diamonds," said the old notary to Paul as he went away.

While waiting for the dancing to begin, whispers went round about the marriage, and doubts were expressed as to the future of the promised couple.

"Is it finally arranged?" said one of the leading personages of the town to Madame Evangelista.

"We had so many documents to read and sign that I fear we are rather late," she replied; "but perhaps we are excusable."

"As for me, I heard nothing," said Natalie, giving her hand to her lover to open the ball.

"Both of those young persons are extravagant, and the mother is not of a kind to check them," said a dowager.

"But they have founded an entail, I am told, worth fifty thousand francs a year."

"Pooh!"

"In that I see the hand of our worthy Monsieur Mathias," said a magistrate. "If it is really true, he has done it to save the future of the family."

"Natalie is too handsome not to be horribly coquettish. After a couple of years of marriage," said one young woman, "I wouldn't answer for Monsieur de Manerville's happiness in his home."

"The Pink of Fashion will then need staking," said Solonet, laughing.

"Don't you think Madame Evangelista looks annoyed?" asked another.

"But, my dear, I have just been told that all she is able to keep is twenty-five thousand francs a year, and what is that to her?"

"Penury!"

"Yes, she has robbed herself for Natalie. Monsieur de Manerville has been so exacting - "

"Extremely exacting," put in Maitre Solonet. "But before long he will be peer of France. The Maulincours and the Vidame de Pamiers will use their influence. He belongs to the faubourg Saint-Germain."

"Oh! he is received there, and that is all," said a lady, who had tried to obtain him as a son-in-law. "Mademoiselle Evangelista, as the daughter of a merchant, will certainly not open the doors of the chapter-house of Cologne to him!"

"She is grand-niece to the Duke of Casa-Reale."

"Through the female line!"

The topic was presently exhausted. The card-players went to the tables, the young people danced, the supper was served, and the ball was not over till morning, when the first gleams of the coming day whitened the windows.

Having said adieu to Paul, who was the last to go away, Madame Evangelista went to her daughter's room; for her own had been taken by the architect to enlarge the scene of the fete. Though Natalie and her mother were overcome with sleep, they said a few words to each other as soon as they were alone.

"Tell me, mother dear, what was the matter with you?"

"My darling, I learned this evening to what lengths a mother's tenderness can go. You know nothing of business, and you are ignorant of the suspicions to which my integrity has been exposed. I have trampled my pride under foot, for your happiness and my reputation were at stake."

"Are you talking of the diamonds? Poor boy, he wept; he did not want them; I have them."

"Sleep now, my child. We will talk business when we wake - for," she added, sighing, "you and I have business now; another person has come between us."

"Ah! my dear mother, Paul will never be an obstacle to our happiness, yours and mine," murmured Natalie, as she went to sleep.

"Poor darling! she little knows that the man has ruined her."

Madame Evangelista's soul was seized at that moment with the first idea of avarice, a vice to which many become a prey as they grow aged. It came into her mind to recover in her daughter's interest the whole of the property left by her husband. She told herself that her honor demanded it. Her devotion to Natalie made her, in a moment, as shrewd and calculating as she had hitherto been careless and wasteful. She resolved to turn her capital to account, after investing a part of it in the Funds, which were then selling at eighty francs. A passion often changes the whole character in a moment; an indiscreet person becomes a diplomatist, a coward is suddenly brave. Hate made this prodigal woman a miser. Chance and luck might serve the project of vengeance, still undefined and confused, which she would now mature in her mind. She fell asleep, muttering to herself, "To-morrow!" By an unexplained phenomenon, the effects of which are familiar to all thinkers, her mind, during sleep, marshalled its ideas, enlightened them, classed them, prepared a means by which she was to rule Paul's life, and showed her a plan which she began to carry out on that very to-morrow.

CHAPTER V

THE MARRIAGE CONTRACT - THIRD DAY

Though the excitement of the fete had driven from Paul's mind the anxious thoughts that now and then assailed it, when he was alone with himself and in his bed they returned to torment him.

"It seems to me," he said to himself, "that without that good Mathias my mother-in-law would have tricked me. And yet, is that believable? What interest could lead her to deceive me? Are we not to join fortunes and live together? Well, well, why should I worry about it? In two days Natalie will be my wife, our money relations are plainly defined, nothing can come between us. Vogue la galere - Nevertheless, I'll be upon my guard. Suppose Mathias was right? Well, if he was, I'm not obliged to marry my mother-in-law."

In this second battle of the contract Paul's future had completely changed in aspect, though he was not aware of it. Of the two persons whom he was marrying, one, the cleverest, was now his mortal enemy, and meditated already withdrawing her interests from the common fund. Incapable of observing the difference that a Creole nature placed between his mother-in-law and other women, Paul was far from suspecting her craftiness. The Creole nature is apart from all others; it derives from Europe by its intellect, from the tropics by the illogical violence of its passions, from the East by the apathetic indifference with which it does, or suffers, either good or evil, equally, - a graceful nature withal, but dangerous, as a child is dangerous if not watched. Like a child, the Creole woman must have her way immediately; like a child, she would burn a house to boil an egg. In her soft and easy life she takes no care upon her mind; but when impassioned, she thinks of all things. She has something of the perfidy of the Negroes by whom she has been surrounded from her cradle, but she is also as naive and even, at times, as artless as they. Like them and like the children, she wishes doggedly for one thing with a growing intensity of desire, and will brood upon that idea until she hatches it. A strange assemblage of virtues and defects! which her Spanish nature had strengthened in Madame Evangelista, and over which her French experience had cast the glaze of its politeness.

This character, slumbering in married happiness for sixteen years, occupied since then with the trivialities of social life, this nature to which a first hatred had revealed its strength, awoke now like a conflagration; at the moment of the woman's life when she was losing the dearest object of her affections and needed another element for the energy that possessed her, this flame burst forth. Natalie could be but three days more beneath her influence! Madame Evangelista, vanquished at other points, had one clear day before her, the last of those that a daughter spends beside her mother. A few words, and the Creole nature could influence the lives of the two beings about to walk together through the brambled paths and the dusty high-roads of Parisian society, for Natalie believed in her mother blindly. What far-reaching power would the counsel of that Creole nature have on a mind so subservient! The whole future of these lives might be determined by one single speech. No code, no human institution can prevent the crime that kills by words. There lies the weakness of social law; in that is the difference between the morals of the great world and the morals of the people: one is frank, the other hypocritical; one employs the knife, the other the venom of ideas and language; to one death, to the other impunity.

The next morning, about mid-day, Madame Evangelista was half seated, half lying on the edge of her daughter's bed. During that waking hour they caressed and played together in happy memory of their loving life; a life in which no discord had ever troubled either the harmony of their feelings, the agreement of their ideas, or the mutual choice and enjoyment of their pleasures.

"Poor little darling!" said the mother, shedding true tears, "how can I help being sorrowful when I think that after I have fulfilled your every wish during your whole life you will belong, to-morrow night, to a man you must obey?"

"Oh, my dear mother, as for obeying! - " and Natalie made a little motion of her head which expressed a graceful rebellion. "You are joking," she continued. "My father always gratified your caprices; and why not? he loved you. And I am loved, too."

"Yes, Paul has a certain love for you. But if a married woman is not careful nothing more rapidly evaporates than conjugal love. The influence a wife ought to have over her husband depends entirely on how she begins with him. You need the best advice."

"But you will be with us."

"Possibly, my child. Last night, while the ball was going on, I reflected on the dangers of our being together. If my presence were to do you harm, if the little acts by which you ought slowly, but surely, to establish your authority as a wife should be attributed to my influence, your home would become a hell. At the first frown I saw upon your husband's brow I, proud as I am, should instantly leave his house. If I were driven to leave it, better, I think, not to enter it. I should never forgive your husband if he caused trouble between us. Whereas, when you have once become the mistress, when your husband is to you what your father was to me, that danger is no longer to be feared. Though this wise policy will cost your young and tender heart a pang, your happiness demands that you become the absolute sovereign of your home."

"Then why, mamma, did you say just now I must obey him?"

"My dear little daughter, in order that a wife may rule, she must always seem to do what her husband wishes. If you were not told this you might by some impulsive opposition destroy your future. Paul is a weak young man; he might allow a friend to rule him; he might even fall under the dominion of some woman who would make you feel her influence. Prevent such disasters by making yourself from the very start his ruler. Is it not better that he be governed by you than by others?"

"Yes, certainly," said Natalie. " I should think only of

his happiness."

"And it is my privilege, darling, to think only of yours, and to wish not to leave you at so crucial a moment without a compass in the midst of the reefs through which you must steer."

"But, dearest mother, are we not strong enough, you and I, to stay together beside him, without having to fear those frowns you seem to dread. Paul loves you, mamma."

"Oh! oh! He fears me more than he loves me. Observe him carefully to-day when I tell him that I shall let you go to Paris without me, and you will see on his face, no matter what pains he takes to conceal it, his inward joy."

"Why should he feel so?"

"Why? Dear child! I am like Saint-Jean Bouche-d'Or. I will tell that to himself, and before you."

"But suppose I marry on condition that you do not leave me?" urged Natalie.

"Our separation is necessary," replied her mother. "Several considerations have greatly changed my future. I am now poor. You will lead a brilliant life in Paris, and I could not live with you suitably without spending the little that remains to me. Whereas, if I go to Lanstrac, I can take care of your property there and restore my fortune by economy."

"You, mamma! *You* practise economy!" cried Natalie, laughing. "Don't begin to be a grandmother yet. What!

do you mean to leave me for such reasons as those? Dear mother, Paul may seem to you a trifle stupid, but he is not one atom selfish or grasping."

"Ah!" replied Madame Evangelista, in a tone of voice big with suggestions which made the girl's heart throb, "those discussions about the contract have made me distrustful. I have my doubts about him - But don't be troubled, dear child," she added, taking her daughter by the neck and kissing her. "I will not leave you long alone. Whenever my return can take place without making difficulty between you, whenever Paul can rightly judge me, we will begin once more our happy little life, our evening confidences -"

"Oh! mother, how can you think of living without your Natalie?"

"Because, dear angel, I shall live for her. My mother's heart will be satisfied in the thought that I contribute, as I ought, to your future happiness."

"But, my dear, adorable mother, must I be alone with Paul, here, now, all at once? What will become of me? what will happen? what must I do? what must I not do?"

"Poor child! do you think that I would utterly abandon you to your first battle? We will write to each other three times a week like lovers. We shall thus be close to each other's hearts incessantly. Nothing can happen to you that I shall not know, and I can save you from all misfortune. Besides, it would be too ridiculous if I never went to see you; it would seem to show dislike or disrespect to your husband; I will always spend a month or two every year with you in Paris."

"Alone, already alone, and with him!" cried Natalie in terror, interrupting her mother.

"But you wish to be his wife?"

"Yes, I wish it. But tell me how I should behave, - you, who did what you pleased with my father. You know the way; I'll obey you blindly."

Madame Evangelista kissed her daughter's forehead. She had willed and awaited this request.

"Child, my counsels must adept themselves to circumstances. All men are not alike. The lion and the frog are not more unlike than one man compared with another, - morally, I mean. Do I know to-day what will happen to you to-morrow? No; therefore I can only give you general advice upon the whole tenor of your conduct."

"Dear mother, tell me, quick, all that you know yourself."

"In the first place, my dear child, the cause of the failure of married women who desire to keep their husbands' hearts - and," she said, making a parenthesis, "to keep their hearts and rule them is one and the same thing - Well, the principle cause of conjugal disunion is to be found in perpetual intercourse, which never existed in the olden time, but which has been introduced into this country of late years with the mania for family. Since the Revolution the manners and customs of the bourgeois have invaded the homes of the aristocracy. This misfortune is due to one of their writers, Rousseau, an infamous heretic, whose ideas were all anti-social and who pretended, I don't know how, to justify the most senseless things. He declared that all women had the same rights and the same faculties; that living in a state of society we ought, nevertheless, to obey nature - as if the wife of a Spanish grandee, as if you or I had anything in common with the women of the people! Since then, well-bred women have suckled their children, have educated their daughters, and stayed in their own homes. Life has become so involved that happiness is almost impossible, - for a perfect harmony between natures such as that which has made you and me live as two friends is an exception. Perpetual contact is as dangerous for parents and children as it is for husband and wife. There are few souls in which love survives this fatal omnipresence. Therefore, I say, erect between yourself and Paul the barriers of society; go to balls and operas; go out in the morning, dine out in the evenings, pay visits constantly, and grant but little of your time to your husband. By this means you will always keep your value to him. When two beings bound together for life have nothing to live upon but sentiment, its resources are soon exhausted, indifference, satiety, and disgust succeed. When sentiment has withered what will become of you? Remember, affection once extinguished can lead to nothing but indifference or contempt. Be ever young and ever new to him. He may weary you, - that often happens, - but you must never weary him. The faculty of being bored without showing it is a condition of all species of power. You cannot diversify happiness by the cares of property or the occupations of a family. If you do not make your husband share your social interests, if you do not keep him amused you will fall into a dismal apathy. Then begins the SPLEEN of love. But a man will always love the woman who amuses him and keeps him happy. To give happiness and to receive it are two lines of feminine conduct which are separated by a gulf."

"Dear mother, I am listening to you, but I don't understand one word you say."

"If you love Paul to the extent of doing all he asks of you, if you make your happiness depend on him, all is over with your future life; you will never be mistress of your home, and the best precepts in the world will do you no good."

"That is plainer; but I see the rule without knowing how to apply it," said Natalie, laughing. "I have the theory; the practice will come."

"My poor Ninie," replied the mother, who dropped an honest tear at the thought of her daughter's marriage, "things will happen to teach it to you - And," she continued, after a pause, during which the mother and daughter held each other closely embraced in the truest sympathy, "remember this, my Natalie: we all have our destiny as women, just as men have their vocation as men. A woman is born to be a woman of the world and a charming hostess, as a man is born to be a general or a poet. Your vocation is to please. Your education has formed you for society. In these days women should be educated for the salon as they once were for the gynoecium. You were not born to be the mother of a family or the steward of a household. If you have children, I hope they will not come to spoil your figure on the morrow of your marriage; nothing is so bourgeois as to have a child at once. If you have them two or three years after your marriage, well and good; governesses and tutors will bring them up. YOU are to be the lady, the great lady, who represents the luxury and the pleasure of the house. But remember one thing - let your superiority be visible in those things only which flatter a man's self-love; hide the superiority you must also acquire over him in great things."

"But you frighten me, mamma," cried Natalie. "How can I remember all these precepts? How shall I ever manage, I, such a child, and so heedless, to reflect and calculate before I act?"

"But, my dear little girl, I am telling you to-day that which you must surely learn later, buying your experience by fatal faults and errors of conduct which will cause you bitter regrets and embarrass your whole life."

"But how must I begin?" asked Natalie, artlessly.

"Instinct will guide you," replied her mother. "At this moment Paul desires you more than he loves you; for love born of desires is a hope; the love that succeeds their satisfaction is the reality. There, my dear, is the question; there lies your power. What woman is not loved before marriage? Be so on the morrow and you shall remain so always. Paul is a weak man who is easily trained to habit. If he yields to you once he will yield always. A woman ardently desired can ask all things; do not commit the folly of many women who do not see the importance of the first hours of their sway, - that of wasting your power on trifles, on silly things with no result. Use the empire your husband's first emotions give you to accustom him to obedience. And when you make him yield, choose that it be on some unreasonable point, so as to test the measure of your power by the measure of his concession. What victory would there be in making him agree to a reasonable thing? Would that be obeying you? We must always, as the Castilian proverb says, take the bull by the horns; when a bull has once seen the inutility of his defence and of his strength he is beaten. When your husband does a foolish thing for you, you can govern him."

"Why so?"

"Because, my child, marriage lasts a lifetime, and a husband is not a man like other men. Therefore, never commit the folly of giving yourself into his power in everything. Keep up a constant reserve in your speech and in your actions. You may even be cold to him without danger, for you can modify coldness at will. Besides, nothing is more easy to maintain than our dignity. The words, 'It is not becoming in your wife to do thus and so,' is a great talisman. The life of a woman lies in the words, 'I will not.' They are the final argument. Feminine power is in them, and therefore they should only be used on real occasions. But they constitute a means of governing far beyond that of argument or discussion. I, my dear child, reigned over your father by his faith in me. If your husband believes in you, you can do all things with him. To inspire that belief you must make him think that you understand him. Do not suppose that that is an easy thing to do. A woman can always make a man think that he is loved, but to make him admit that he is understood is far more difficult. I am bound to tell you all now, my child, for to-morrow life with its complications, life with two wills which *must* be made one, begins for you. Bear in mind, at all moments, that difficulty. The only means of harmonizing your two wills is to arrange from the first that there shall be but one; and that will must be yours. Many persons declare that a wife creates her own unhappiness by changing sides in this way; but, my dear, she can only become the mistress by controlling events instead of bearing them; and that advantage compensates for any difficulty."

Natalie kissed her mother's hands with tears of gratitude. Like all women in whom mental emotion is never warmed by physical emotion, she suddenly comprehended the bearings of this feminine policy; but, like a spoiled child that never admits the force of reason and returns obstinately to its one desire, she came back to the charge with one of those personal arguments which the logic of a child suggests: -

"Dear mamma," she said, "it is only a few days since you were talking of Paul's advancement, and saying that you alone could promote it; why, then, do you suddenly turn round and abandon us to ourselves?"

"I did not then know the extent of my obligations nor the amount of my debts," replied the mother, who would not suffer her real motive to be seen. "Besides, a year or two hence I can take up that matter again. Come, let us dress; Paul will be here soon. Be as sweet and caressing as you were, - you know? - that night when we first discussed this fatal contract; for to-day we must save the last fragments of our fortune, and I must win for you a thing to which I am superstitiously attached."

"What is it?"

"The 'Discreto.'"

Paul arrived about four o'clock. Though he endeavored to meet his mother-in-law with a gracious look upon his face, Madame Evangelista saw traces of the clouds which the counsels of the night and the reflections of the morning had brought there.

"Mathias has told him!" she thought, resolving to defeat the old notary's action. "My dear son," she said, "you left your diamonds in the drawer of the console, and I frankly confess that I would rather not see again the things that threatened to bring a cloud between us. Besides, as Monsieur Mathias said, they ought to be sold at once to meet the first payment on the estates you have purchased."

"They are not mine," he said. "I have given them to Natalie, and when you see them upon her you will forget the pain they caused you."

Madame Evangelista took his hand and pressed it cordially, with a tear of emotion.

"Listen to me, my dear children," she said, looking from Paul to Natalie; "since you really feel thus, I have a proposition to make to both of you. I find myself obliged to sell my pearl necklace and my earrings. Yes, Paul, it is necessary; I do not choose to put a penny of my fortune into an annuity; I know what I owe to you. Well, I admit a weakness; to sell the 'Discreto' seems to me a disaster. To sell a diamond which bears the name of Philip the Second and once adorned his royal hand, an historic stone which the Duke of Alba touched for ten years in the hilt of his sword - no, no, I cannot! Elie Magus estimates my necklace and ear-rings at a hundred and some odd thousand francs without the clasps. Will you exchange the other jewels I made over to you for these? you will gain by the transaction, but what of that? I am not selfish. Instead of those mere fancy jewels, Paul, your wife will have fine diamonds which she can really enjoy. Isn't it better that I should sell those ornaments which will surely go out of fashion, and that you should keep in the family these priceless stones?"

"But, my dear mother, consider yourself," said Paul.

"I," replied Madame Evangelista, "I want such things no longer. Yes, Paul, I am going to be your bailiff at Lanstrac. It would be folly in me to go to Paris at the moment when I ought to be here to liquidate my property and settle my affairs. I shall grow miserly for my grandchildren."

"Dear mother," said Paul, much moved, "ought I to accept this exchange without paying you the difference?"

"Good heavens! are you not, both of you, my dearest interests? Do you suppose I shall not find happiness in thinking, as I sit in my chimney-corner, 'Natalie is dazzling to-night at the Duchesse de Berry's ball'? When she sees my diamond at her throat and my ear-rings in her ears she will have one of those little enjoyments of vanity which contribute so much to a woman's happiness and make her so gay and fascinating. Nothing saddens a woman more than to have her vanity repressed; I have never seen an ill-dressed woman who was amiable or good-humored."

"Heavens! what was Mathias thinking about?" thought Paul. "Well, then, mamma," he said, in a low voice, "I accept."

"But I am confounded!" said Natalie.

At this moment Solonet arrived to announce the good news that he had found among the speculators of Bordeaux two contractors who were much attracted by the house, the gardens of which could be covered with dwellings.

"They offer two hundred and fifty thousand francs," he said; "but if you consent to the sale, I can make them give you three hundred thousand. There are three acres of land in the garden."

"My husband paid two hundred thousand for the place, therefore I consent," she replied. "But you must reserve the furniture and the mirrors."

"Ah!" said Solonet, "you are beginning to understand business."

"Alas! I must," she said, sighing.

"I am told that a great many persons are coming to your midnight service," said Solonet, perceiving that his presence was inopportune, and preparing to go.

Madame Evangelista accompanied him to the door of the last salon, and there she said, in a low voice: -

"I now have personal property to the amount of two hundred and fifty thousand francs; if I can get two hundred thousand for my share of the house it will make a handsome capital, which I shall want to invest to the very best advantage. I count on you for that. I shall probably live at Lanstrac."

The young notary kissed his client's hand with a gesture of gratitude; for the widow's tone of voice made Solonet fancy that this alliance, really made from self-interest only, might extend a little farther.

"You can count on me," he replied. "I can find you investments in merchandise on which you will risk nothing and make very considerable profits."

"Adieu until to-morrow," she said; "you are to be our witness, you know, with Monsieur le Marquis de Gyas."

"My dear mother," said Paul, when she returned to them, "why do you refuse to come to Paris? Natalie is provoked with me, as if I were the cause of your decision."

"I have thought it all over, my children, and I am sure that I should hamper you. You would feel obliged to make me a third in all you did, and young people have ideas of their own which I might, unintentionally, thwart. Go to Paris. I do not wish to exercise over the Comtesse de Manerville the gentle authority I have held over Natalie. I desire to leave her wholly to you. Don't you see, Paul, that there are habits and ways between us which must be broken up? My influence ought to yield to yours. I want you to love me, and to believe that I have your interests more at heart than you think for. Young husbands are, sooner or later, jealous for the love of a wife for her mother. Perhaps they are right. When you are thoroughly united, when love has blended your two souls into one, then, my dear son, you will not fear an opposing influence if I live in your house. I know the world, and men, and things; I have seen the peace of many a home destroyed by the blind love of mothers who made themselves in the end as intolerable to their daughters as to their sons-in-law. The affection of old people is often exacting and querulous. Perhaps I could not efface myself as I should. I have the weakness to think myself still handsome; I have flatterers who declare that I am still agreeable; I should have, I fear, certain pretensions which might interfere with your lives. Let me, therefore, make one more sacrifice for your happiness. I have given you my fortune, and now I desire to resign to you my last vanities as a woman. Your notary Mathias is getting old. He cannot look after your estates as I will. I will be your bailiff; I will create for myself those natural occupations which are the pleasures of old age. Later, if necessary, I will come to you in Paris, and second you in your projects of ambition. Come, Paul, be frank; my proposal suits you, does it not?"

Paul would not admit it, but he was at heart delighted to get his liberty. The suspicions which Mathias had put into his mind respecting his mother-in-law were, however, dissipated by this conversation, which Madame Evangelista carried on still longer in the same tone.

"My mother was right," thought Natalie, who had watched Paul's countenance. "He *is* glad to know that I am separated from her - why?"

That "why" was the first note of a rising distrust; did it prove the power of those maternal instructions?

There are certain characters which on the faith of a single proof believe in friendship. To persons thus constituted the north wind drives away the clouds as rapidly as the south wind brings them; they stop at effects and never hark back to causes. Paul had one of those essentially confiding natures, without ill-feelings, but also without foresight. His weakness proceeded far more from his kindness, his belief in goodness, than from actual debility of soul.

Natalie was sad and thoughtful, for she knew not what to do without her mother. Paul, with that self-confident conceit which comes of love, smiled to himself at her sadness, thinking how soon the pleasures of marriage and the excitements of Paris would drive it away. Madame Evangelista saw this confidence with much satisfaction. She had already taken two great steps. Her daughter possessed the diamonds which had cost Paul two hundred thousand francs; and she had gained her point of leaving these two children to themselves with no other guide than their illogical love. Her revenge was thus preparing, unknown to her daughter, who would, sooner or later, become its accomplice. Did Natalie love Paul? That was a question still undecided, the answer to which might modify her projects, for she loved her daughter too sincerely not to respect her happiness. Paul's future, therefore, still depended on himself. If he could make his wife love him, he was saved.

The next day, at midnight, after an evening spent together, with the addition of the four witnesses, to whom Madame Evangelista gave the formal dinner which follows the legal marriage, the bridal pair, accompanied by their friends, heard mass by torch-light, in presence of a crowd of inquisitive persons. A marriage celebrated at night always suggests to the mind an unpleasant omen. Light is the symbol of life and pleasure, the forecasts of which are lacking to a midnight wedding. Ask the intrepid soul why it shivers; why the chill of those black arches enervates it; why the sound of steps startles it; why it notices the cry of bats and the hoot of owls. Though there is absolutely no reason to tremble, all present do tremble, and the darkness, emblem of death, saddens them. Natalie, parted from her mother, wept. The girl was now a prey to those doubts which grasp the heart as it enters a new career in which, despite all assurances of happiness, a thousand pitfalls await the steps of a young wife. She was cold and wanted a mantle. The air and manner of Madame Evangelista and that of the bridal pair excited some comment among the elegant crowd which surrounded the altar.

"Solonet tells me that the bride and bridegroom leave for Paris to-morrow morning, all alone."

"Madame Evangelista was to live with them, I thought."

"Count Paul has got rid of her already."

"What a mistake!" said the Marquise de Gyas. "To shut the door on the mother of his wife is to open it to a lover. Doesn't he know what a mother is?"

"He has been very hard on Madame Evangelista; the poor woman has had to sell her house and her diamonds, and is going to live at Lanstrac."

"Natalie looks very sad."

"Would you like to be made to take a journey the day after your marriage?"

"It is very awkward."

"I am glad I came here to-night," said a lady. "I am now convinced of the necessity of the pomps of marriage and of wedding fetes; a scene like this is very bare and sad. If I may say what I think," she added, in a whisper to her neighbor, "this marriage seems to me indecent."

Madame Evangelista took Natalie in her carriage and accompanied her, alone, to Paul's house.

"Well, mother, it is done!"

"Remember, my dear child, my last advice, and you will be a happy woman. Be his wife, and not his mistress."

When Natalie had retired, the mother played the little comedy of flinging herself with tears into the arms of her son-in-law. It was the only provincial thing that Madame Evangelista allowed herself, but she had her reasons for it. Amid tears and speeches, apparently half wild and despairing, she obtained of Paul those concessions which all husbands make.

The next day she put the married pair into their carriage, and accompanied them to the ferry, by which the road to Paris crosses the Gironde. With a look and a word Natalie enabled her mother to see that if Paul had won the trick in the game of the contract, her revenge was beginning. Natalie was already reducing her husband to perfect obedience.

CHAPTER VI

CONCLUSION

Five years later, on an afternoon in the month of November, Comte Paul de Manerville, wrapped in a cloak, was entering, with a bowed head and a mysterious manner, the house of his old friend Monsieur Mathias at Bordeaux.

Too old to continue in business, the worthy notary had sold his practice and was ending his days peacefully in a quiet house to which he had retired. An urgent affair had obliged him to be absent at the moment of his guest's arrival, but his housekeeper, warned of Paul's coming, took him to the room of the late Madame Mathias, who had been dead a year. Fatigued by a rapid journey, Paul slept till evening. When the old man reached home he went up to his client's room, and watched him sleeping, as a mother watches her child. Josette, the old housekeeper, followed her master and stood before the bed, her hands on her hips.

"It is a year to-day, Josette, since I received my dear wife's last sigh; I little knew then that I should stand here again to see the count half dead."

"Poor man! he moans in his sleep," said Josette.

"Sac a papier!" cried the old notary, an innocent oath which was a sign with him of the despair on a man of business before insurmountable difficulties. "At any rate," he thought, "I have saved the title to the Lanstrac estate for him, and that of Ausac, Saint-Froult, and his house, though the usufruct has gone." Mathias counted his fingers. "Five years! Just five years this month, since his old aunt, now dead, that excellent Madame de Maulincour, asked for the hand of that little crocodile of a woman, who has finally ruined him - as I expected."

And the gouty old gentleman, leaning on his cane, went to walk in the little garden till his guest should awake. At nine o'clock supper was served, for Mathias took supper. The old man was not a little astonished, when Paul joined him, to see that his old client's brow was calm and his face serene, though noticeably changed. If at the age of thirty-three the Comte de Manerville seemed to be a man of forty, that change in his appearance was due solely to mental shocks; physically, he was well. He clasped the old man's hand affectionately, and forced him not to rise, saying: -

"Dear, kind Maitre Mathias, you, too, have had your troubles."

"Mine were natural troubles, Monsieur le comte; but yours - "

"We will talk of that presently, while we sup."

"If I had not a son in the magistracy, and a daughter married," said the good old man, "you would have found in old Mathias, believe me, Monsieur le comte, something better than mere hospitality. Why have you come to Bordeaux at the very moment when posters are on all the walls of the seizure of your farms at Grassol and Guadet, the vineyard of Belle-Rose and the family mansion? I cannot tell you the grief I feel at the sight of those placards, - I, who for forty years nursed that property as if it belonged to me; I, who bought it for your mother when I was only third clerk to Monsieur Chesnau, my predecessor, and wrote the deeds myself in my best round hand; I, who have those titles now in my successor's office; I, who have known you since you were so high"; and the old man stopped to put his hand near the ground. "Ah! a man must have been a notary for forty-one years and a half to know the sort of grief I feel to see my name exposed before the face of Israel in those announcements of the seizure and sale of the property. When I pass through the streets and see men reading these horrible yellow posters, I am ashamed, as if my own honor and ruin were concerned. Some fools will stand there and read them aloud expressly to draw other fools about them - and what imbecile remarks they make! As if a man were not master of his own property! Your father ran through two fortunes before he made the one he left you; and you wouldn't be a Manerville if you didn't do likewise. Besides, seizures of real estate have a whole section of the Code to themselves; they are expected and provided for; you are in a position recognized by the law. - If I were not an old man with white hair, I would thrash those fools I hear reading aloud in the streets such an abomination as this," added the worthy notary, taking up a paper; "'At the request of Dame Natalie Evangelista, wife of Paul-Francois-Joseph, Comte de Manerville, separated from him as to worldly goods and chattels by the Lower court of the department of the Seine - '"

"Yes, and now separated in body," said Paul.

"Ah!" exclaimed the old man.

"Oh! against my wife's will," added the count, hastily. "I was forced to deceive her; she did not know that I was leaving her."

"You have left her?"

"My passage is taken; I sail for Calcutta on the 'Belle-Amelie.'"

"Two day's hence!" cried the notary. "Then, Monsieur le comte, we shall never meet again."

"You are only seventy-three, my dear Mathias, and you have the gout, the brevet of old age. When I return I shall find you still afoot. Your good head and heart will be as sound as ever, and you will help me to reconstruct what is now a shaken edifice. I intend to make a noble fortune in seven years. I shall be only forty on my return. All is still possible at that age."

"You?" said Mathias, with a gesture of amazement, - you, Monsieur le comte, to undertake commerce! How can you even think of it?"

"I am no longer Monsieur le comte, dear Mathias. My passage is taken under the name of Camille, one of my mother's baptismal names. I have acquirements which will enable me to make my fortune otherwise than in business. Commerce, at any rate, will be only my final chance. I start with a sum in hand sufficient for the redemption of my future on a large scale."

"Where is that money?"

"A friend is to send it to me."

The old man dropped his fork as he heard the word "friend," not in surprise, not scoffingly, but in grief; his look and manner expressed the pain he felt in finding Paul under the influence of a deceitful illusion; his practised eye fathomed a gulf where the count saw nothing but solid ground.

"I have been fifty years in the notariat," he said, "and I never yet knew a ruined man whose friend would lend him money."

"You don't know de Marsay. I am certain that he has sold out some of his investments already, and to-morrow you will receive from him a bill of exchange for one hundred and fifty thousand francs."

"I hope I may. If that be so, cannot your friend settle your difficulties here? You could live quietly at Lanstrac for five or six years on your wife's income, and so recover yourself."

"No assignment or economy on my part could pay off fifteen hundred thousand francs of debt, in which my wife is involved to the amount of five hundred and fifty thousand."

"You cannot mean to say that in four years you have incurred a million and a half of debt?"

"Nothing is more certain, Mathias. Did I not give those diamonds to my wife? Did I not spend the hundred and fifty thousand I received from the sale of Madame

Evangelista's house, in the arrangement of my house in Paris? Was I not forced to use other money for the first payments on that property demanded by the marriage contract? I was even forced to sell out Natalie's forty thousand a year in the Funds to complete the purchase of Auzac and Saint-Froult. We sold at eighty-seven, therefore I became in debt for over two hundred thousand francs within a month after my marriage. That left us only sixty-seven thousand francs a year; but we spent fully three times as much every year. Add all that up, together with rates of interest to usurers, and you will soon find a million."

"Br-r-r!" exclaimed the old notary. "Go on. What next?"

"Well, I wanted, in the first place, to complete for my wife that set of jewels of which she had the pearl necklace clasped by the family diamond, the 'Discreto,' and her mother's ear-rings. I paid a hundred thousand francs for a coronet of diamond wheat-ears. There's eleven hundred thousand. And now I find I owe the fortune of my wife, which amounts to three hundred and sixty-six thousand francs of her 'dot.'"

"But," said Mathias, "if Madame la comtesse had given up her diamonds and you had pledged your income you could have pacified your creditors and have paid them off in time."

"When a man is down, Mathias, when his property is covered with mortgages, when his wife's claims take precedence of his creditors', and when that man has notes out for a hundred thousand francs which he must pay (and I hope I can do so out of the increased value of my property here), what you propose is not possible."

"This is dreadful!" cried Mathias; "would you sell Belle-Rose with the vintage of 1825 still in the cellars?"

"I cannot help myself."

"Belle-Rose is worth six hundred thousand francs."

"Natalie will buy it in; I have advised her to do so."

"I might push the price to seven hundred thousand, and the farms are worth a hundred thousand each."

"Then if the house in Bordeaux can be sold for two hundred thousand - "

"Solonet will give more than that; he wants it. He is retiring with a handsome property made by gambling on the Funds. He has sold his practice for three hundred thousand francs, and marries a mulatto woman. God knows how she got her money, but they say it amounts to millions. A notary gambling in stocks! a notary marrying a black woman! What an age! It is said that he speculates for your mother-in-law with her funds."

"She has greatly improved Lanstrac and taken great pains with its cultivation. She has amply repaid me for the use of it."

"I shouldn't have thought her capable of that."

"She is so kind and so devoted; she has always paid Natalie's debts during the three months she spent with us every year in Paris."

"She could well afford to do so, for she gets her living out of Lanstrac," said Mathias. "She! grown economical! what a miracle! I am told she has just bought the domain of Grainrouge between Lanstrac and Grassol; so that if the Lanstrac avenue were extended to the high-road, you would drive four and a half miles through your own property to reach the house. She paid one hundred thousand francs down for Grainrouge."

"She is as handsome as ever," said Paul; "country life preserves her freshness; I don't mean to go to Lanstrac and bid her good-bye; her heart would bleed for me too much."

"You would go in vain; she is now in Paris. She probably arrived there as you left."

"No doubt she had heard of the sale of my property and came to help me. I have no complaint to make of life, Mathias. I am truly loved, - as much as any man ever could be here below; beloved by two women who outdo each other in devotion; they are even jealous of each other; the daughter blames the mother for loving me too much, and the mother reproaches the daughter for what she calls her dissipations. I may say that this great affection has been my ruin. How could I fail to satisfy even the slightest caprice of a loving wife? Impossible to restrain myself! Neither could I accept any sacrifice on her part. We might certainly, as you say, live at Lanstrac, save my income, and part with her diamonds, but I would rather go to India and work for a fortune than tear my Natalie from the life she enjoys. So it was I who proposed the separation as to property. Women are angels who ought not to be mixed up in the sordid interests of life."

Old Mathias listened in doubt and amazement.

"You have no children, I think," he said.

"Fortunately, none," replied Paul.

"That is not my idea of marriage," remarked the old notary, naively. "A wife ought, in my opinion, to share the good and evil fortunes of her husband. I have heard that young married people who love like lovers, do not want children? Is pleasure the only object of marriage? I say that object should be the joys of family. Moreover, in this case - I am afraid you will think me too much of notary - your marriage contract made it incumbent upon you to have a son. Yes, monsieur le comte, you ought to have had at once a male heir to consolidate that entail. Why not? Madame Evangelista was strong and healthy; she had nothing to fear in maternity. You will tell me, perhaps, that these are the old-fashioned notions of our ancestors. But in those noble families, Monsieur le comte, the legitimate wife thought it her duty to bear children and bring them up nobly; as the Duchesse de Sully, the wife of the great Sully, said, a wife is not an instrument of pleasure, but the honor and virtue of her household."

"You don't know women, my good Mathias," said Paul. "In order to be happy we must love them as they want to be loved. Isn't there something brutal in at once depriving a wife of her charms, and spoiling her beauty before she has begun to enjoy it?"

"If you had had children your wife would not have

dissipated your fortune; she would have stayed at home and looked after them."

"If you were right, dear friend," said Paul, frowning, "I should be still more unhappy than I am. Do not aggravate my sufferings by preaching to me after my fall. Let me go, without the pang of looking backward to my mistakes."

The next day Mathias received a bill of exchange for one hundred and fifty thousand francs from de Marsay.

"You see," said Paul, "he does not write a word to me. He begins by obliging me. Henri's nature is the most imperfectly perfect, the most illegally beautiful that I know. If you knew with what superiority that man, still young, can rise above sentiments, above self-interests, and judge them, you would be astonished, as I am, to find how much heart he has."

Mathias tried to battle with Paul's determination, but he found it irrevocable, and it was justified by so many cogent reasons that the old man finally ceased his endeavors to retain his client.

It is seldom that vessels sail promptly at the time appointed, but on this occasion, by a fateful circumstance for Paul, the wind was fair and the "Belle-Amelie" sailed on the morrow, as expected. The quay was lined with relations, and friends, and idle persons. Among them were several who had formerly known Manerville. His disaster, posted on the walls of the town, made him as celebrated as he was in the days of his wealth and fashion. Curiosity was aroused; every one had their word to say about him. Old Mathias accompanied his client to the quay, and his sufferings were sore as he caught a few words of those remarks: -

"Who could recognize in that man you see over there, near old Mathias, the dandy who was called the Pink of Fashion five years ago, and made, as they say, 'fair weather and foul' in Bordeaux."

"What! that stout, short man in the alpaca overcoat, who looks like a groom, - is that Comte Paul de Manerville?"

"Yes, my dear, the same who married Mademoiselle Evangelista. Here he is, ruined, without a penny to his name, going out to India to look for luck."

"But how did he ruin himself? he was very rich."

"Oh! Paris, women, play, luxury, gambling at the Bourse - "

"Besides," said another, "Manerville always was a poor creature; no mind, soft as papier-mache, he'd let anybody shear the wool from his back; incapable of anything, no matter what. He was born to be ruined."

Paul wrung the hand of the old man and went on board. Mathias stood upon the pier, looking at his client, who leaned against the shrouds, defying the crowed before him with a glance of contempt. At the moment when the sailors began to weigh anchor, Paul noticed that Mathias was making signals to him with his handkerchief. The old housekeeper had hurried to her master, who seemed to be excited by some sudden event. Paul asked the captain to wait a moment, and send a boat to the pier, which was done. Too feeble himself to go aboard, Mathias gave two letters to a sailor in the boat.

"My friend," he said, "this packet" (showing one of the two letters) "is important; it has just arrived by a courier from Paris in thirty-five hours. State this to Monsieur le comte; don't neglect to do so; it may change his plans."

"Would he come ashore?"

"Possibly, my friend," said the notary, imprudently.

The sailor is, in all lands, a being of a race apart, holding all land-folk in contempt. This one happened to be a bas-Breton, who saw but one thing in Maitre Mathias's request.

"Come ashore, indeed!" he thought, as he rowed. "Make the captain lose a passenger! If one listened to those walruses we'd have nothing to do but embark and disembark 'em. He's afraid that son of his will catch cold."

The sailor gave Paul the letter and said not a word of the message. Recognizing the handwriting of his wife and de Marsay, Paul supposed that he knew what they both would urge upon him. Anxious not to be influenced by offers which he believed their devotion to his welfare would inspire, he put the letters in his pocket unread, with apparent indifference.

Absorbed in the sad thoughts which assail the strongest man under such circumstances, Paul gave way to his grief as he waved his hand to his old friend, and bade farewell to France, watching the steeples of Bordeaux as they fled out of sight. He seated himself on a coil of rope. Night overtook him still lost in thought. With the semi-darkness of the dying day came doubts; he cast an anxious eye into the future. Sounding it, and finding there uncertainty and danger, he asked his soul if courage would fail him. A vague dread seized his mind as he thought of Natalie left wholly to herself; he repented the step he had taken; he regretted Paris and his life there. Suddenly sea-sickness overcame him. Every one knows the effect of that disorder. The most horrible of its sufferings devoid of danger is a complete dissolution of the will. An inexplicable distress relaxes to their very centre the cords of vitality; the soul no longer performs its functions; the sufferer becomes indifferent to everything; the mother forgets her child, the lover his mistress, the strongest man lies prone, like an inert mass. Paul was carried to his cabin, where he stayed three days, lying on his back, gorged with grog by the sailors, or vomiting; thinking of nothing, and sleeping much. Then he revived into a species of convalescence, and returned by degrees to his ordinary condition. The first morning after he felt better he went on deck and passed the poop, breathing in the salt breezes of another atmosphere. Putting his hands into his pockets he felt the letters. At once he opened them, beginning with that of his wife.

In order that the letter of the Comtesse de Manerville be fully understood, it is necessary to give the one which Paul had written to her on the day that he left Paris.

From Paul de Manerville to his wife:

My beloved, - When you read this letter I shall be far away from you; perhaps already on the vessel which is to take me to India, where I am going to repair my shattered fortune.

I have not found courage to tell you of my departure. I have deceived you; but it was best to do so. You would only have been uselessly distressed; you would have wished to sacrifice your fortune, and that I could not have suffered. Dear Natalie, feel no remorse; I have no regrets. When I return with millions I shall imitate your father and lay them at your feet, as he laid his at the feet of your mother, saying to you: "All I have is yours."

I love you madly, Natalie; I say this without fear that the avowal will lead you to strain a power which none but weak men fear; yours has been boundless from the day I knew you first. My love is the only accomplice in my disaster. I have felt, as my ruin progressed, the delirious joys of a gambler; as the money diminished, so my enjoyment grew. Each fragment of my fortune turned into some little pleasure for you gave me untold happiness. I could have wished that you had more caprices that I might gratify them all. I knew I was marching to a precipice, but I went on crowned with joys of which a common heart knows nothing. I have acted like those lovers who take refuge in a cottage on the shores of some lake for a year or two, resolved to kill themselves at last; dying thus in all the glory of their illusions and their love. I have always thought such persons infinitely sensible.

You have known nothing of my pleasures or my sacrifices. The greatest joy of all was to hide from the one beloved the cost of her desires. I can reveal these secrets to you now, for when you hold this paper, heavy with love, I shall be far away. Though I lose the treasures of your gratitude, I do not suffer that contraction of the heart which would disable me if I spoke to you of these matters. Besides, my own beloved, is there not a tender calculation in thus revealing to you the history of the past? Does it not extend our love into the future? - But we need no such supports! We love each other with a love to which proof is needless, - a love which takes no note of time or distance, but lives of itself alone.

Ah! Natalie, I have just looked at you asleep, trustful, restful as a little child, your hand stretched toward me. I left a tear upon the pillow which has known our precious joys. I leave you without fear, on the faith of that attitude; I go to win the future of our love by bringing home to you a fortune large enough to gratify your every taste, and let no shadow of anxiety disturb our joys. Neither you nor I can do without enjoyments in the life we live. To me belongs the task of providing the necessary fortune. I am a man; and I have courage.

Perhaps you might seek to follow me. For that reason I conceal from you the name of the vessel, the port from which I sail, and the day of sailing. After I am gone, when too late to follow me, a friend will tell you all.

Natalie! my affection is boundless. I love you as a mother loves her child, as a lover loves his mistress, with absolute unselfishness. To me the toil, to you the pleasures; to me all sufferings, to you all happiness. Amuse yourself; continue your habits of luxury; go to theatres and operas, enjoy society and balls; I leave you free for all things. Dear angel, when you return to this nest where for five years we have tasted the fruits which love has ripened think of your friend; think for a moment of me, and rest upon my heart.

That is all I ask of you. For myself, dear eternal thought of mine! whether under burning skies, toiling for both of us, I face obstacles to vanquish, or whether, weary with the struggle, I rest my mind on hopes of a return, I shall think of you alone; of you who are my life, - my blessed life! Yes, I shall live in you. I shall tell myself daily that you have no troubles, no cares; that you are happy. As in our natural lives of day and night, of sleeping and waking, I shall have sunny days in Paris, and nights of toil in India, - a painful dream, a joyful reality; and I shall live so utterly in that reality that my actual life will pass as a dream. I shall have memories! I shall recall, line by line, strophe by strophe, our glorious five years' poem. I shall remember the days of your pleasure in some new dress or some adornment which made you to my eyes a fresh delight. Yes, dear angel, I go like a man vowed to some great emprize, the guerdon of which, if success attend him, is the recovery of his beautiful mistress. Oh! my precious love, my Natalie, keep me as a religion in your heart. Be the child that I have just seen asleep! If you betray my confidence, my blind confidence, you need not fear my anger - be sure of that; I should die silently. But a wife does not deceive the man who leaves her free - for woman is never base. She tricks a tyrant; but an easy treachery, which would kill its victim, she will not commit - No, no! I will not think of it. Forgive this cry, this single cry, so natural to the heart of man!

Dear love, you will see de Marsay; he is now the lessee of our house, and he will leave you in possession of it. This nominal lease was necessary to avoid a useless loss. Our creditors, ignorant that their payment is a question of time only, would otherwise have seized the furniture and the temporary possession of the house. Be kind to de Marsay; I have the most entire confidence in his capacity and his loyalty. Take him as your defender and adviser, make him your slave. However occupied, he will always find time to be devoted to you. I have placed the liquidation of my affairs and the payment of the debts in his hands. If he should advance some sum of which he should later feel in need I rely on you to pay it back. Remember, however, that I do not leave you to de Marsay, but *to yourself*; I do not seek to impose him upon you.

Alas! I have but an hour more to stay beside you; I cannot spend that hour in writing business - I count your breaths; I try to guess your thoughts in the slight motions of your sleep. I would I could infuse my blood into your veins that you might be a part of me, my thought your thought, and your heart mine - A murmur has just escaped your lips as though it were a soft reply. Be calm and beautiful forever as you are now! Ah! would that I possessed that fabulous fairy power which, with a wand, could make you sleep while I am absent, until, returning, I should wake you with a kiss.

How much I must love you, how much energy of soul I must possess, to leave you as I see you now! Adieu, my cherished one. Your poor Pink of Fashion is blown away by stormy winds, but - the wings of his good luck shall waft him back to you.

No, my Ninie, I am not bidding you farewell, for I shall never leave you. Are you not the soul of my actions? Is not the hope of returning with happiness indestructible for YOU the end and aim of my endeavor? Does it not lead my every step? You will be with me everywhere. Ah! it will not be the sun of India, but the fire of your eyes that lights my way. Therefore be happy - as happy as a woman can be without her lover. I would the last kiss that I take from those dear lips were not a passive one; but, my Ninie, my adored one, I will not wake you. When you wake, you will find a tear upon your forehead - make it a talisman! Think, think of him who may, perhaps, die for you, far from you; think less of the husband than of the lover who confides you to God.

From the Comtesse de Manerville to her husband:

Dear, beloved one, - Your letter has plunged me into affliction. Had you the right to take this course, which must affect us equally, without consulting me? Are you free? Do you not belong to me? If you must go, why should I not follow you? You show me, Paul, that I am not indispensable to you. What have I done, to be deprived of my rights? Surely I count for something in this ruin. My luxuries have weighed somewhat in the scale. You make me curse the happy, careless life we have led for the last five years. To know that you are banished from France for years is enough to kill me. How soon can a fortune be made in India? Will you ever return?

I was right when I refused, with instinctive obstinacy, that separation as to property which my mother and you were so determined to carry out. What did I tell you then? Did I not warn you that it was casting a reflection upon you, and would ruin your credit? It was not until you were really angry that I gave way.

My dear Paul, never have you been so noble in my eyes as you are at this moment. To despair of nothing, to start courageously to seek a fortune! Only your character, your strength of mind could do it. I sit at your feet. A man who avows his weakness with your good faith, who rebuilds his fortune from the same motive that made him wreck it, for love's sake, for the sake of an irresistible passion, oh, Paul, that man is sublime! Therefore, fear nothing; go on, through all obstacles, not doubting your Natalie - for that would be doubting yourself. Poor darling, you mean to live in me? And I shall ever be in you. I shall not be here; I shall be wherever you are, wherever you go.

Though your letter has caused me the keenest pain, it has also filled me with joy - you have made me know those two extremes! Seeing how you love me, I have been proud to learn that my love is truly felt. Sometimes I have thought that I loved you more than you loved me. Now, I admit myself vanquished, you have added the delightful superiority - of loving - to all the others with which you are blest. That precious letter in which your soul reveals itself will lie upon my heart during all your absence; for my soul, too, is in it; that letter is my glory.

I shall go to live at Lanstrac with my mother. I die to the world; I will economize my income and pay your debts to their last farthing. From this day forth, Paul, I am another woman. I bid farewell forever to society; I will have no pleasures that you cannot share. Besides, Paul, I ought to leave Paris and live in retirement. Dear friend, you will soon have a noble reason to make your fortune. If your courage needed a spur you would find it in this. Cannot you guess? We shall have a child. Your cherished desires are granted. I feared to give you one of those false hopes which hurt so much - have we not had grief enough already on that score? I was determined not to be mistaken in this good news. To-day I feel certain, and it makes me happy to shed this joy upon your sorrows.

This morning, fearing nothing and thinking you still at home, I went to the Assumption; all things smiled upon me; how could I foresee misfortune? As I left the church I met my mother; she had heard of your distress, and came, by post, with all her savings, thirty thousand francs, hoping to help you. Ah! what a heart is hers, Paul! I felt joyful, and hurried home to tell you this good news, and to breakfast with you in the greenhouse, where I ordered just the dainties that you like. Well, Augustine brought me your letter, - a letter from you, when we had slept together! A cold fear seized me; it was like a dream! I read your letter! I read it weeping, and my mother shared my tears. I was half-dead. Such love, such courage, such happiness, such misery! The richest fortunes of the heart, and the momentary ruin of all interests! To lose you at a moment when my admiration of your greatness thrilled me! what woman could have resisted such a tempest of emotion? To know you far away when your hand upon my heart would have stilled its throbbings; to feel that YOU were not here to give me that look so precious to me, to rejoice in our new hopes; that I was not with you to soften your sorrows by those caresses which made your Natalie so dear to you! I wished to start, to follow you, to fly to you. But my mother told me you had taken passage in a ship which leaves Bordeaux to-morrow, that I could not reach you except by post, and, moreover, that it was madness in my present state to risk our future by attempting to follow you. I could not bear such violent emotions; I was taken ill, and am writing to you now in bed.

My mother is doing all she can to stop certain calumnies which seem to have got about on your disaster. The Vandenesses, Charles and Felix, have earnestly defended you; but your friend de Marsay treats the affair satirically. He laughs at your accusers instead of replying to them. I do not like his way of lightly brushing aside such serious attacks. Are you not deceived in him? However, I will obey you; I will make him my friend. Do not be anxious, my adored one, on the points that concern your honor; is it not mine as well? My diamonds shall be pledged; we intend, mamma and I, to employ our utmost resources in the payment of your debts; and we shall try to buy back your vineyard at Belle-Rose. My mother, who understands business like a lawyer, blames you very much for not having told her of your embarrassments. She would not have bought - thinking to please you - the Grainrouge domain, and then she could have lent you that money as well as the thirty thousand francs she brought with her. She is in despair at your decision; she fears the climate of India for your health. She entreats you to be sober, and not to let yourself be trapped by women - That made me laugh; I am as sure of you as I am of myself. You will return to me rich and faithful. I alone know your feminine delicacy, and the secret sentiments which make you a human flower worthy of the gardens of heaven. The Bordeaux people were right when they gave you your floral nickname.

But alas! who will take care of my delicate flower? My heart is rent with dreadful ideas. I, his wife, Natalie, I am here, and perhaps he suffers far away from me! And not to share your pains, your vexations, your dangers! In whom will you confide? how will you live without that ear into which you have hitherto poured all? Dear, sensitive plant, swept away by this storm, will you be able to survive in another soil than your native land?

It seems to me that I have been alone for centuries. I have wept sorely. To be the cause of your ruin! What a text for the thoughts of a loving woman! You treated me like a child to whom we give all it asks, or like a courtesan, allowed by some thoughtless youth to squander his fortune. Ah! such indulgence was, in truth, an insult. Did you think I could not live without fine dresses, balls and operas and social triumphs? Am I so frivolous a woman? Do you think me incapable of serious thought, of ministering to your fortune as I have to your pleasures? If you were not so far away, and so unhappy, I would blame you for that impertinence. Why lower your wife in that way? Good heavens! what induced me to go into society at all? - to flatter your vanity; I adorned myself for you, as you well know. If I did wrong, I am punished, cruelly; your absence is a harsh expiation of our mutual life.

Perhaps my happiness was too complete; it had to

be paid by some great trial - and here it is. There is nothing now for me but solitude. Yes, I shall live at Lanstrac, the place your father laid out, the house you yourself refurnished so luxuriously. There I shall live, with my mother and my child, and await you, - sending you daily, night and morning, the prayers of all. Remember that our love is a talisman against all evil. I have no more doubt of you than you can have of me. What comfort can I put into this letter, - I so desolate, so broken, with the lonely years before me, like a desert to cross. But no! I am not utterly unhappy; the desert will be brightened by our son, - yes, it must be a *son*, must it not?

And now, adieu, my own beloved; our love and prayers will follow you. The tears you see upon this paper will tell you much that I cannot write. I kiss you on this little square of paper, see! below. Take those kisses from

Your Natalie.

This letter threw Paul into a reverie caused as much by memories of the past as by these fresh assurances of love. The happier a man is, the more he trembles. In souls which are exclusively tender - and exclusive tenderness carries with it a certain amount of weakness - jealousy and uneasiness exist in direct proportion to the amount of the happiness and its extent. Strong souls are neither jealous nor fearful; jealousy is doubt, fear is meanness. Unlimited belief is the principal attribute of a great man. If he is deceived (for strength as well as weakness may make a man a dupe) his contempt will serve him as an axe with which to cut through all. This greatness, however, is the exception. Which of us has not known what it is to be abandoned by the spirit which sustains our frail machine, and to hearken to that mysterious Voice denying all? Paul, his mind going over the past, and caught here and there by irrefutable facts, believed and doubted all. Lost in thought, a prey to an awful and involuntary incredulity, which was combated by the instincts of his own pure love and his faith in Natalie, he read and re-read that wordy letter, unable to decide the question which it raised either for or against his wife. Love is sometimes as great and true when smothered in words as it is in brief, strong sentences.

To understand the situation into which Paul de Manerville was about to enter we must think of him as he was at this moment, floating upon the ocean as he floated upon his past, looking back upon the years of his life as he looked at the limitless water and cloudless sky about him, and ending his reverie by returning, through tumults of doubt, to faith, the pure, unalloyed and perfect faith of the Christian and the lover, which enforced the voice of his faithful heart.

It is necessary to give here his own letter to de Marsay written on leaving Paris, to which his friend replied in the letter he received through old Mathias from the dock: -

From Comte Paul de Manerville to Monsieur le Marquis Henri de Marsay:

> Henri, - I have to say to you one of the most vital words a man can say to his friend: - I am ruined. When you read this I shall be on the point of sailing from Bordeaux to Calcutta on the brig "Belle-Amelie."

You will find in the hands of your notary a deed which only needs your signature to be legal. In it, I lease my house to you for six years at a nominal rent. Send a duplicate of that deed to my wife. I am forced to take this precaution that Natalie may continue to live in her own home without fear of being driven out by creditors.

I also convey to you by deed the income of my share of the entailed property for four years; the whole amounting to one hundred and fifty thousand francs, which sum I beg you to lend me and to send in a bill of exchange on some house in Bordeaux to my notary, Maitre Mathias. My wife will give you her signature to this paper as an endorsement of your claim to my income. If the revenues of the entail do not pay this loan as quickly as I now expect, you and I will settle on my return. The sum I ask for is absolutely necessary to enable me to seek my fortune in India; and if I know you, I shall receive it in Bordeaux the night before I sail.

I have acted as you would have acted in my place. I held firm to the last moment, letting no one suspect my ruin. Before the news of the seizure of my property at Bordeaux reached Paris, I had attempted, with one hundred thousand francs which I obtained on notes, to recover myself by play. Some lucky stroke might still have saved me. I lost.

How have I ruined myself? By my own will, Henri. From the first month of my married life I saw that I could not keep up the style in which I started. I knew the result; but I chose to shut my eyes; I could not say to my wife, "We must leave Paris and live at Lanstrac." I have ruined myself for her as men ruin themselves for a mistress, but I knew it all along. Between ourselves, I am neither a fool nor a weak man. A fool does not let himself be ruled with his eyes open by a passion; and a man who starts for India to reconstruct his fortune, instead of blowing out his brains, is not weak.

I shall return rich, or I shall never return at all. Only, my dear friend, as I want wealth solely for *her*, as I must be absent six years at least, and as I will not risk being duped in any way, I confide to you my wife. I know no better guardian. Being childless, a lover might be dangerous to her. Henri! I love her madly, basely, without proper pride. I would forgive her, I think, an infidelity, not because I am certain of avenging it, but because I would kill myself to leave her free and happy - since I could not make her happiness myself. But what have I to fear? Natalie feels for me that friendship which is independent of love, but which preserves love. I have treated her like a petted child. I took such delight in my sacrifices, one led so naturally to another, that she can never be false; she would be a monster if she were. Love begets love.

Alas! shall I tell you all, my dear Henri? I have just written her a letter in which I let her think that I go with heart of hope and brow serene; that neither jealousy, nor doubt, nor fear is in my soul, - a letter, in short, such as a son might write to his mother, aware that he is going to his death. Good God! de Marsay, as I wrote it hell was in my soul! I am the most wretched man on earth. Yes, yes, to you the cries, to you the grinding of my teeth! I avow myself to you a despairing lover; I would rather live these six years sweeping the streets beneath her windows than return a millionaire at the end of them - if I could choose. I suffer agony; I shall pass from pain to pain until I hear from you that you will take the trust which you alone can fulfil or accomplish.

Oh! my dear de Marsay, this woman is indispensable to my life; she is my sun, my atmosphere. Take her under your shield and buckler, keep her faithful to me, even if she wills it not. Yes, I could be satisfied with a half-happiness. Be her guardian, her chaperon, for I could have no distrust of you. Prove to her that in betraying me she would do a low and vulgar thing, and be no better than the common run of women; tell her that faithfulness will prove her lofty spirit.

She probably has fortune enough to continue her life of luxury and ease. But if she lacks a pleasure, if she has caprices which she cannot satisfy, be her banker, and do not fear, I *will* return with wealth.

But, after all, these fears are in vain! Natalie is an angel of purity and virtue. When Felix de Vandenesse fell deeply in love with her and began to show her certain attentions, I had only to let her see the danger, and she instantly thanked me so affectionately that I was moved to tears. She said that her dignity and reputation demanded that she should not close her doors abruptly to any man, but that she knew well how to dismiss him. She did, in fact, receive him so coldly that the affair all ended for the best. We have never had any other subject of dispute - if, indeed, a friendly talk could be called a dispute - in all our married life.

And now, my dear Henri, I bid you farewell in the spirit of a man. Misfortune has come. No matter what the cause, it is here. I strip to meet it. Poverty and Natalie are two irreconcilable terms. The balance may be close between my assets and my liabilities, but no one shall have cause to complain of me. But, should any unforeseen event occur to imperil my honor, I count on you.

Send letters under cover to the Governor of India at Calcutta. I have friendly relations with his family, and some one there will care for all letters that come to me from Europe. Dear friend, I hope to find you the same de Marsay on my return, - the man who scoffs at everything and yet is receptive of the feelings of others when they accord with the grandeur he is conscious of in himself. You stay in Paris, friend; but when you read these words, I shall be crying out, "To Carthage!"

The Marquis Henri de Marsay to Comte Paul de Manerville:

So, so, Monsieur le comte, you have made a wreck of it! Monsieur l'ambassadeur has gone to the bottom! Are these the fine things that you were doing?

Why, Paul, why have you kept away from me? If you had said a single word, my poor old fellow, I would have made your position plain to you. Your wife has refused me her endorsement. May that one word unseal your eyes! But, if that does not suffice, learn that your notes have been protested at the instigation of a Sieur Lecuyer, formerly head-clerk to Maitre Solonet, a notary in Bordeaux. That usurer in embryo (who came from Gascony for jobbery) is the proxy of your very honorable mother-in-law, who is the actual holder of your notes for one hundred thousand francs, on which I am told that worthy woman doled out to you only seventy thousand. Compared with Madame Evangelista, papa Gobseck is flannel, velvet, vanilla cream, a sleeping draught. Your vineyard of Belle-Rose is to fall into the clutches of your wife, to whom her mother pays the difference between the price it goes for at the auction sale and the amount of her dower claim upon it. Madame Evangelista will also have the farms at Guadet and Grassol, and the mortgages on your house in Bordeaux already belong to her, in the names of straw men provided by Solonet.

Thus these two excellent women will make for themselves a united income of one hundred and twenty thousand francs a year out of your misfortunes and forced sale of property, added to the revenue of some thirty-odd thousand on the Grand-livre which these cats already possess.

The endorsement of your wife was not needed; for this morning the said Sieur Lecuyer came to offer me a return of the sum I had lent you in exchange for a legal transfer of my rights. The vintage of 1825 which your mother-in-law keeps in the cellars at Lanstrac will suffice to pay me.

These two women have calculated, evidently, that you are now upon the ocean; but I send this letter by courier, so that you may have time to follow the advice I now give you.

I made Lecuyer talk. I disentangled from his lies,

his language, and his reticence, the threads I lacked to bring to light the whole plot of the domestic conspiracy hatched against you. This evening, at the Spanish embassy, I shall offer my admiring compliments to your mother-in-law and your wife. I shall pay court to Madame Evangelista; I intend to desert you basely, and say sly things to your discredit, - nothing openly, or that Mascarille in petticoats would detect my purpose. How did you make her such an enemy? That is what I want to know. If you had had the wit to be in love with that woman before you married her daughter, you would to-day be peer of France, Duc de Manerville, and, possibly, ambassador to Madrid.

If you had come to me at the time of your marriage, I would have helped you to analyze and know the women to whom you were binding yourself; out of our mutual observations safety might have been yours. But, instead of that, these women judged me, became afraid of me, and separated us. If you had not stupidly given in to them and turned me the cold shoulder, they would never have been able to ruin you. Your wife brought on the coldness between us, instigated by her mother, to whom she wrote two letters a week, - a fact to which you paid no attention. I recognized my Paul when I heard that detail.

Within a month I shall be so intimate with your mother-in-law that I shall hear from her the reasons of the hispano-italiano hatred which she feels for you, - for you, one of the best and kindest men on earth! Did she hate you before her daughter fell in love with Felix de Vandenesse; that's a question in my mind. If I had not taken a fancy to go to the East with Montriveau, Ronquerolles, and a few other good fellows of your acquaintance, I should have been in a position to tell you something about that affair, which was beginning just as I left Paris. I saw the first gleams even then of your misfortune. But what gentleman is base enough to open such a subject unless appealed to? Who shall dare to injure a woman, or break that illusive mirror in which his friend delights in gazing at the fairy scenes of a happy marriage? Illusions are the riches of the heart.

Your wife, dear friend, is, I believe I may say, in the fullest application of the word, a fashionable woman. She thinks of nothing but her social success, her dress, her pleasures; she goes to opera and theatre and balls; she rises late and drives to the Bois, dines out, or gives a dinner-party. Such a life seems to me for women very much what war is for men; the public sees only the victors; it forgets the dead. Many delicate women perish in this conflict; those who come out of it have iron constitutions, consequently no heart, but good stomachs. There lies the reason of the cold insensibility of social life. Fine souls keep themselves reserved, weak and tender natures succumb; the rest are cobblestones which hold the social organ in its place, water-worn and rounded by the tide, but never worn-out. Your wife has maintained that life with ease; she looks made for it; she is always fresh and beautiful. To my mind the deduction is plain, - she has never loved you; and you have loved her like a madman.

To strike out love from that siliceous nature a man of iron was needed. After standing, but without enduring, the shock of Lady Dudley, Felix was the fitting mate to Natalie. There is no great merit in divining that to you she was indifferent. In love with her yourself, you have been incapable of perceiving the cold nature of a young woman whom you have fashioned and trained for a man like Vandenesse. The coldness of your wife, if you perceived it, you set down, with the stupid jurisprudence of married people, to the honor of her reserve and her innocence. Like all husbands, you thought you could keep her virtuous in a society where women whisper from ear to ear that which men are afraid to say.

No, your wife has liked the social benefits she derived from marriage, but the private burdens of it she found rather heavy. Those burdens, that tax was - you! Seeing nothing of all this, you have gone on digging your abysses (to use the hackneyed words of rhetoric) and covering them with flowers. You have mildly obeyed the law which rules the ruck of men; from which I desired to protect you. Dear fellow! only one thing was wanting to make you as dull as the bourgeois deceived by his wife, who is all astonishment or wrath, and that is that you should talk to me of your sacrifices, your love for Natalie, and chant that psalm: "Ungrateful would she be if she betrayed me; I have done this, I have done that, and more will I do; I will go to the ends of the earth, to the Indies for her sake. I - I - " etc. My dear Paul, have you never lived in Paris, have you never had the honor of belonging by ties of friendship to Henri de Marsay, that you should be so ignorant of the commonest things, the primitive principles that move the feminine mechanism, the a-b-c of their hearts? Then hear me: -

Suppose you exterminate yourself, suppose you go to Saint-Pelagie for a woman's debts, suppose you kill a score of men, desert a dozen women, serve like Laban, cross the deserts, skirt the galleys, cover yourself with glory, cover yourself with shame, refuse, like Nelson, to fight a battle until you have kissed the shoulder of Lady Hamilton, dash yourself, like Bonaparte, upon the bridge at Arcola, go mad like Roland, risk your life to dance five minutes with a woman - my dear fellow, what have all those things to do with *love*? If love were won by samples such as those mankind would be too happy. A spurt of prowess at the moment of desire would give a man the woman that he wanted. But love, *love*, my good Paul, is a faith like that in the Immaculate conception of the Holy Virgin; it comes, or it does not come. Will the mines of Potosi, or the shedding of our blood, or the making of our fame serve to waken an involuntary, an inexplicable sentiment? Young men like you, who expect to be loved as the balance of your account, are nothing else than usurers. Our legitimate wives owe us virtue and children, but they don't owe us love.

Love, my dear Paul, is the sense of pleasure given and received, and the certainty of giving and receiving it; love is a desire incessantly moving and growing, incessantly satisfied and insatiable. The day when Vandenesse stirred the cord of a desire in your wife's heart which you had left untouched, all your self-satisfied affection, your gifts, your deeds, your money, ceased to be even memories; one emotion of love in your wife's heart has cast out the treasures of your own passion, which are now nothing better than old iron. Felix has the virtues and the beauties in her eyes, and the simple moral is that blinded by your own love you never made her love you.

Your mother-in-law is on the side of the lover against the husband, - secretly or not; she may have closed her eyes, or she may have opened them; I know not what she has done - but one thing is certain, she is for her daughter, and against you. During the fifteen years that I have observed society, I have never yet seen a mother who, under such circumstances, abandons her daughter. This indulgence seems to be an inheritance transmitted in the female line. What man can blame it? Some copyist of the Civil code, perhaps, who sees formulas only in the place of feelings.

As for your present position, the dissipation into which the life of a fashionable woman cast you, and your own easy nature, possibly your vanity, have opened the way for your wife and her mother to get rid of you by this ruin so skilfully contrived. From all of which you will conclude, my good friend, that the mission you entrusted to me, and which I would all the more faithfully fulfil because it amused me, is, necessarily, null and void. The evil you wish me to prevent is accomplished, - "consummatum est."

Forgive me, dear friend, if I write to you, as you say, a la de Marsay on subjects which must seem to you very serious. Far be it from me to dance upon the grave of a friend, like heirs upon that of a progenitor. But you have written to me that you mean to act the part of a man, and I believe you; I therefore treat you as a man of the world, and not as a lover. For you, this blow ought to be like the brand on the shoulder of a galley-slave, which flings him forever into a life of systematic opposition to society. You are now freed of one evil; marriage possessed you; it now behooves you to turn round and possess marriage.

Paul, I am your friend in the fullest acceptation of the word. If you had a brain in an iron skull, if you had the energy which has come to you too late, I would have proved my friendship by telling you things that would have made you walk upon humanity as upon a carpet. But when I did talk to you guardedly of Parisian civilization, when I told you in the disguise of fiction some of the actual adventures of my youth, you regarded them as mere romance and would not see their bearing. When I told you that history of a lawyer at the galleys branded for forgery, who committed the crime to give his wife, adored like yours, an income of thirty thousand francs, and whom his wife denounced that she might be rid of him and free to love another man, you exclaimed, and other fools who were supping with us exclaimed against me. Well, my dear Paul, you were that lawyer, less the galleys.

Your friends here are not sparing you. The sister of the two Vandenesses, the Marquise de Listomere and all her set, in which, by the bye, that little Rastignac has enrolled himself, - the scamp will make his way! - Madame d'Aiglemont and her salon, the Lenoncourts, the Comtesse Ferraud, Madame d'Espard, the Nucingens, the Spanish ambassador, in short, all the cliques in society are flinging mud upon you. You are a bad man, a gambler, a dissipated fellow who has squandered his property. After paying your debts a great many times, your wife, an angel of virtue, has just redeemed your notes for one hundred thousand francs, although her property was separate from yours. Luckily, you had done the best you could do by disappearing. If you had stayed here you would have made her bed in the straw; the poor woman would have been the victim of her conjugal devotion!

When a man attains to power, my dear Paul, he has all the virtues of an epitaph; let him fall into poverty, and he has more sins than the Prodigal Son; society at the present moment gives you the vices of a Don Juan. You gambled at the Bourse, you had licentious tastes which cost you fabulous sums of money to gratify; you paid enormous interests to money-lenders. The two Vandenesses have told everywhere how Gigonnet gave you for six thousand francs an ivory frigate, and made your valet buy it back for three hundred in order to sell it to you again. The incident did really happen to Maxime de Trailles about nine years ago; but it fits your present circumstances so well that Maxime has forever lost the command of his frigate.

In short, I can't tell you one-half that is said; you have supplied a whole encyclopaedia of gossip which the women have an interest in swelling. Your wife is having an immense success. Last evening at the opera Madame Firmiani began to repeat to me some of the things that are being said. "Don't talk of that," I replied. "You know nothing of the real truth, you people. Paul has robbed the Bank, cheated the Treasury, murdered Ezzelin and three Medoras in the rue Saint-Denis, and I think, between ourselves, that he is a member of the Dix-Mille. His associate is the famous Jacques Collin, on whom the police have been unable to lay a hand since he escaped from the galleys. Paul gave him a room in his house; you see he is capable of anything; in fact, the two have gone off to India together to rob the Great Mogul." Madame Firmiani, like the distinguished woman that she is, saw that she ought not to convert her beautiful lips into a mouthpiece for false denunciation.

Many persons, when they hear of these tragi-comedies of life, refuse to believe them. They take the side of human nature and fine sentiments; they declare that these things do not exist. But Talleyrand said a fine thing, my dear fellow: "All things happen." Truly, things happen under our very noses which are more amazing than this domestic plot of yours; but society has an interest in denying them, and in declaring itself calumniated. Often these dramas are played so naturally and with such a varnish of good taste that even I have to rub the lens of my opera-glass to see to the bottom of them. But, I repeat to you, when a man is a friend of mine, when we have received together the baptism of champagne and have knelt together before the altar of the Venus Commodus, when the crooked fingers of play have given us their benediction, if that man finds himself in a false position I'd ruin a score of families to do him justice.

You must be aware from all this that I love you. Have I ever in my life written a letter as long as this? No. Therefore, read with attention what I still have to say.

Alas! Paul, I shall be forced to take to writing, for I

am taking to politics. I am going into public life. I intend to have, within five years, the portfolio of a ministry or some embassy. There comes an age when the only mistress a man can serve is his country. I enter the ranks of those who intend to upset not only the ministry, but the whole present system of government. In short, I swim in the waters of a certain prince who is lame of the foot only, - a man whom I regard as a statesman of genius whose name will go down to posterity; a prince as complete in his way as a great artist may be in his.

Several of us, Ronquerolles, Montriveau, the Grandlieus, La Roche-Hugon, Serisy, Feraud, and Granville, have allied ourselves against the "parti-pretre," as the party-ninny represented by the "Constitutionnel" has ingeniously said. We intend to overturn the Navarreins, Lenoncourts, Vandenesses, and the Grand Almonry. In order to succeed we shall even ally ourselves with Lafayette, the Orleanists, and the Left, - people whom we can throttle on the morrow of victory, for no government in the world is possible with their principles. We are capable of anything for the good of the country - and our own.

Personal questions as to the King's person are mere sentimental folly in these days; they must be cleared away. From that point of view, the English with their sort of Doge, are more advanced than we are. Politics have nothing to do with that, my dear fellow. Politics consist in giving the nation an impetus by creating an oligarchy embodying a fixed theory of government, and able to direct public affairs along a straight path, instead of allowing the country to be pulled in a thousand different directions, which is what has been happening for the last forty years in our beautiful France - at once so intelligent and so sottish, so wise and so foolish; it needs a system, indeed, much more than men. What are individuals in this great question? If the end is a great one, if the country may live happy and free from trouble, what do the masses care for the profits of our stewardship, our fortune, privileges, and pleasures?

I am now standing firm on my feet. I have at the present moment a hundred and fifty thousand francs a year in the Three per Cents, and a reserve of two hundred thousand francs to repair damages. Even this does not seem to me very much ballast in the pocket of a man starting left foot foremost to scale the heights of power.

A fortunate accident settled the question of my setting out on this career, which did not particularly smile on me, for you know my predilection for the life of the East. After thirty-five years of slumber, my highly-respected mother woke up to the recollection that she had a son who might do her honor. Often when a vine-stock is eradicated, some years after shoots come up to the surface of the ground; well, my dear boy, my mother had almost torn me up by the roots from her heart, and I sprouted again in her head. At the age of fifty-eight, she thinks herself old enough to think no more of any men but her son. At this juncture she has met in some hot-water cauldron, at I know not what baths, a delightful old maid - English, with two hundred and forty thousand francs a year; and, like a good mother, she has inspired her with an audacious ambition to become my wife. A maid of six-and-thirty, my word! Brought up in the strictest puritanical principles, a steady sitting hen, who maintains that unfaithful wives should be publicly burnt. 'Where will you find wood enough?' I asked her. I could have sent her to the devil, for two hundred and forty thousand francs a year are no equivalent for liberty, nor a fair price for my physical and moral worth and my prospects. But she is the sole heiress of a gouty old fellow, some London brewer, who within a calculable time will leave her a fortune equal at least to what the sweet creature has already. Added to these advantages, she has a red nose, the eyes of a dead goat, a waist that makes one fear lest she should break into three pieces if she falls down, and the coloring of a badly painted doll. But - she is delightfully economical; but - she will adore her husband, do what he will; but - she has the English gift; she will manage my house, my stables, my servants, my estates better than any steward. She has all the dignity of virtue; she holds herself as erect as a confidante on the stage of the Francais; nothing will persuade me that she has not been impaled and the shaft broken off in her body. Miss Stevens is, however, fair enough to be not too unpleasing if I must positively marry her. But - and this to me is truly pathetic - she has the hands of a woman as immaculate as the sacred ark; they are so red that I have not yet hit on any way to whiten them that will not be too costly, and I have no idea how to fine down her fingers, which are like sausages. Yes; she evidently belongs to the brewhouse by her hands, and to the aristocracy by her money; but she is apt to affect the great lady a little too much, as rich English women do who want to be mistaken for them, and she displays her lobster's claws too freely.

She has, however, as little intelligence as I could wish in a woman. If there were a stupider one to be found, I would set out to seek her. This girl, whose name is Dinah, will never criticise me; she will never contradict me; I shall be her Upper Chamber, her Lords and Commons. In short, Paul, she is indefeasible evidence of the English genius; she is a product of English mechanics brought to their highest pitch of perfection; she was undoubtedly made at Manchester, between the manufactory of Perry's pens and the workshops for steam-engines. It eats, it drinks, it walks, it may have children, take good care of them, and bring them up admirably, and it apes a woman so well that you would believe it real.

When my mother introduced us, she had set up the machine so cleverly, had so carefully fitted the pegs, and oiled the wheels so thoroughly, that nothing jarred; then, when she saw I did not make a very wry face, she set the springs in motion, and the woman spoke. Finally, my mother uttered the decisive words, "Miss Dinah Stevens spends no more than thirty thousand francs a year, and has been traveling for seven years in order to economize." - So there is another image, and that one is silver.

Matters are so far advanced that the banns are to be published. We have got as far as "My dear love." Miss makes eyes at me that might floor a porter. The settlements are prepared. My fortune is not inquired into; Miss Stevens devotes a portion of hers to creating an entail in landed estate, bearing an income of two hundred and forty thousand francs, and to the purchase of a house, likewise entailed. The settlement credited to me is of a million francs. She has nothing to complain of. I leave her uncle's money untouched.

The worthy brewer, who has helped to found the entail, was near bursting with joy when he heard that his niece was to be a marquise. He would be capable of doing something handsome for my eldest boy.

I shall sell out of the funds as soon as they are up to eighty, and invest in land. Thus, in two years I may look to get six hundred thousand francs a year out of real estate. So, you see, Paul, I do not give my friends advice that I am not ready to act upon.

If you had but listened to me, you would have an English wife, some Nabob's daughter, who would leave you the freedom of a bachelor and the independence necessary for playing the whist of ambition. I would concede my future wife to you if you were not married already. But that cannot be helped, and I am not the man to bid you chew the cud of the past.

All this preamble was needful to explain to you that for the future my position in life will be such as a man needs if he wants to play the great game of pitch-and-toss. I cannot do without you, my friend. Now, then, my dear Paul, instead of setting sail for India you would do a much wiser thing to navigate with me the waters of the Seine. Believe me, Paris is still the place where fortune, abundant fortune, can be won. Potosi is in the rue Vivienne, the rue de la Paix, the Place Vendome, the rue de Rivoli. In all other places and countries material works and labors, marches and counter-marches, and sweatings of the brow are necessary to the building up of fortune; but in Paris *thought* suffices. Here, every man even mentally mediocre, can see a mine of wealth as he puts on his slippers, or picks his teeth after dinner, in his down-sitting and his up-rising. Find me another place on the globe where a good round stupid idea brings in more money, or is sooner understood than it is here.

If I reach the top of the ladder, as I shall, am I the man to refuse you a helping hand, an influence, a signature? We shall want, we young roues, a faithful friend on whom to count, if only to compromise him and make him a scape-goat, or send him to die like a common soldier to save his general. Government is impossible without a man of honor at one's side, in whom to confide and with whom we can do and say everything.

Here is what I propose. Let the "Belle-Amelie" sail without you; come back here like a thunderbolt; I'll arrange a duel for you with Vandenesse in which you shall have the first shot, and you can wing him like a pigeon. In France the husband who shoots his rival becomes at once respectable and respected. No one ever cavils at him again. Fear, my dear fellow, is a valuable social element, a means of success for those who lower their eyes before the gaze of no man living. I who care as little to live as to drink a glass of milk, and who have never felt the emotion of fear, I have remarked the strange effects produced by that sentiment upon our modern manners. Some men tremble to lose the enjoyments to which they are attached, others dread to leave a woman. The old adventurous habits of other days when life was flung away like a garment exist no longer. The bravery of a great many men is nothing more than a clever calculation on the fear of their adversary. The Poles are the only men in Europe who fight for the pleasure of fighting; they cultivate the art for the art's sake, and not for speculation.

Now hear me: kill Vandenesse, and your wife trembles, your mother-in-law trembles, the public trembles, and you recover your position, you prove your grand passion for your wife, you subdue society, you subdue your wife, you become a hero. Such is France. As for your embarrassments, I hold a hundred thousand francs for you; you can pay your principal debts, and sell what property you have left with a power of redemption, for you will soon obtain an office which will enable you by degrees to pay off your creditors. Then, as for your wife, once enlightened as to her character you can rule her. When you loved her you had no power to manage her; not loving her, you will have an unconquerable force. I will undertake, myself, to make your mother-in-law as supple as a glove; for you must recover the use of the hundred and fifty thousand francs a year those two women have squeezed out of you.

Therefore, I say, renounce this expatriation which seems to me no better than a pan of charcoal or a pistol to your head. To go away is to justify all calumnies. The gambler who leaves the table to get his money loses it when he returns; we must have our gold in our pockets. Let us now, you and I, be two gamblers on the green baize of politics;

between us loans are in order. Therefore take post-horses, come back instantly, and renew the game. You'll win it with Henri de Marsay for your partner, for Henri de Marsay knows how to will, and how to strike.

See how we stand politically. My father is in the British ministry; we shall have close relations with Spain through the Evangelistas, for, as soon as your mother-in-law and I have measured claws she will find there is nothing to gain by fighting the devil. Montriveau is our lieutenant-general; he will certainly be minister of war before long, and his eloquence will give him great ascendancy in the Chamber. Ronquerolles will be minister of State and privy-councillor; Martial de la Roche-Hugon is minister to Germany and peer of France; Serisy leads the Council of State, to which he is indispensable; Granville holds the magistracy, to which his sons belong; the Grandlieus stand well at court; Ferraud is the soul of the Gondreville coterie, - low intriguers who are always on the surface of things, I'm sure I don't know why. Thus supported, what have we to fear? The money question is a mere nothing when this great wheel of fortune rolls for us. What is a woman? - you are not a schoolboy. What is life, my dear fellow, if you let a woman be the whole of it? A boat you can't command, without a rudder, but not without a magnet, and tossed by every wind that blows. Pah!

The great secret of social alchemy, my dear Paul, is to get the most we can out of each age of life through which we pass; to have and to hold the buds of our spring, the flowers of our summer, the fruits of our autumn. We amused ourselves once, a few good fellows and I, for a dozen or more years, like mousquetaires, black, red, and gray; we denied ourselves nothing, not even an occasional filibustering here and there. Now we are going to shake down the plums which age and experience have ripened. Be one of us; you shall have your share in the *pudding* we are going to cook.

Come; you will find a friend all yours in the skin of

H. de Marsay.

As Paul de Manerville ended the reading of this letter, which fell like the blows of a pickaxe on the edifice of his hopes, his illusions, and his love, the vessel which bore him from France was beyond the Azores. In the midst of this utter devastation a cold and impotent anger laid hold of him.

"What had I done to them?" he said to himself.

That is the question of fools, of feeble beings, who, seeing nothing, can nothing foresee. Then he cried aloud: "Henri! Henri!" to his loyal friend. Many a man would have gone mad; Paul went to bed and slept that heavy sleep which follows immense disasters, - the sleep that seized Napoleon after Waterloo.

ADDENDUM

The following personages appear in other stories of the Human Comedy.

Casa-Real, Duc de
The Quest of the Absolute

Claes, Josephine de Temninck, Madame
The Quest of the Absolute

Magus, Elie
The Vendetta
A Bachelor's Establishment
Pierre Grassou
Cousin Pons

Manerville, Paul Francois-Joseph, Comte de
The Thirteen
The Ball at Sceaux
Lost Illusions
A Distinguished Provincial at Paris

Manerville, Comtesse Paul de
The Lily of the Valley
A Daughter of Eve

Marsay, Henri de
The Thirteen

The Unconscious Humorists
Another Study of Woman
The Lily of the Valley
Father Goriot
Jealousies of a Country Town
Ursule Mirouet
Lost Illusions
A Distinguished Provincial at Paris
Letters of Two Brides
The Ball at Sceaux
Modeste Mignon
The Secrets of a Princess
The Gondreville Mystery
A Daughter of Eve

Maulincour, Baronne de
The Thirteen

Stevens, Dinah
Cousin Pons

Vandenesse, Comte Felix de
The Lily of the Valley
Lost Illusions
A Distinguished Provincial at Paris
Cesar Birotteau
Letters of Two Brides
A Start in Life
The Secrets of a Princess
Another Study of Woman
The Gondreville Mystery
A Daughter of Eve

Choose from Thousands of 1stWorldLibrary Classics By

Adolphus WilliamWard
Aesop
Agatha Christie
Alexander Aaronsohn
Alexander Kielland
Alexandre Dumas
Alfred Gatty
Alfred Ollivant
Alice Duer Miller
Alice Turner Curtis
Alice Dunbar
Ambrose Bierce
Amelia E. Barr
Andrew Lang
Andrew McFarland Davis
Anna Sewell
Annie Besant
Annie Hamilton Donnell
Annie Payson Call
Anton Chekhov
Arnold Bennett
Arthur Conan Doyle
Arthur Ransome
Atticus
B. M. Bower
Basil King
Bayard Taylor
Ben Macomber
Booth Tarkington
Bram Stoker
C. Collodi
C. E. Orr
C. M. Ingleby
Carolyn Wells
Catherine Parr Traill
Charles A. Eastman
Charles Dickens
Charles Dudley Warner
Charles Farrar Browne
Charles Ives
Charles Kingsley
Charles Lathrop Pack
Charles Whibley
Charles Willing Beale
Charlotte M. Braeme
Charlotte M.Yonge
Clair W. Hayes
Clarence Day Jr.
Clarence E. Mulford
Clemence Housman
Confucius
Cornelis DeWitt Wilcox
Cyril Burleigh
D. H. Lawrence
Daniel Defoe
David Garnett
Don Carlos Janes
Donald Keyhole
Dorothy Kilner
Dougan Clark
E. Nesbit
E.P.Roe
E. Phillips Oppenheim
Edgar Allan Poe
Edgar Rice Burroughs
Edith Wharton
Edward J. O'Biren
John Cournos
Edwin L. Arnold
Eleanor Atkins
Elizabeth Cleghorn
Gaskell
Elizabeth Von Arnim
Ellem Key
Emily Dickinson
Erasmus W. Jones
Ernie Howard Pie
Ethel Turner
Ethel Watts Mumford
Eugenie Foa
Eugene Wood
Evelyn Everett-Green
Everard Cotes
F. J. Cross
Federick Austin Ogg
Ferdinand Ossendowski
Francis Bacon
Francis Darwin
Frances Hodgson Burnett
Frank Gee Patchin
Frank Harris
Frank Jewett Mather
Frank L. Packard
Frederick Trevor Hill
Frederick Winslow Taylor
Friedrich Kerst
Friedrich Nietzsche
Fyodor Dostoyevsky
Gabrielle E. Jackson
Garrett P. Serviss
Gaston Leroux
George Ade
Geroge Bernard Shaw
George Ebers
George Eliot
George MacDonald
George Orwell
George Tucker
George W. Cable
George Wharton James
Gertrude Atherton
Grace E. King
Grant Allen
Guillermo A. Sherwell
Gulielma Zollinger
Gustav Flaubert
H. A. Cody
H. B. Irving
H. G. Wells
H. H. Munro
H. Irving Hancock
H. Rider Haggard
H. W. C. Davis
Hamilton Wright Mabie
Hans Christian Andersen
Harold Avery
Harold McGrath
Harriet Beecher Stowe
Harry Houidini
Helent Hunt Jackson
Helen Nicolay
Hendy David Thoreau
Henrik Ibsen
Henry Adams
Henry Ford
Henry Frost
Henry James
Henry Jones Ford
Henry Seton Merriman
Henry Wadsworth
Longfellow
Henry W Longfellow
Herbert A. Giles
Herbert N. Casson
Herman Hesse
Homer
Honore De Balzac

Horace Walpole
Horatio Alger, Jr.
Howard Pyle
Howard R. Garis
Hugh Lofting
Hugh Walpole
Humphry Ward
Ian Maclaren
Israel Abrahams
J.G.Austin
J. Henri Fabre
J. M. Barrie
J. Macdonald Oxley
J. S. Knowles
J. Storer Clouston
Jack London
Jacob Abbott
James Allen
James Lane Allen
James Andrews
James Baldwin
James DeMille
James Joyce
James Oliver Curwood
James Oppenheim
James Otis
Jane Austen
Jens Peter Jacobsen
Jerome K. Jerome
John Burroughs
John F. Kennedy
John Gay
John Glasworthy
John Habberton
John Joy Bell
John Milton
John Philip Sousa
Jonathan Swift
Joseph Carey
Joseph Conrad
Joseph Jacobs
Julian Hawthrone
Julies Vernes
Justin Huntly McCarthy
Kakuzo Okakura
Kenneth Grahame
Kate Langley Bosher
L. A. Abbot
L. T. Meade
L. Frank Baum
Laura Lee Hope
Laurence Housman
Leo Tolstoy
Leonid Andreyev
Lewis Carroll
Lilian Bell
Lloyd Osbourne
Louis Tracy
Louisa May Alcott
Lucy Fitch Perkins
Lucy Maud Montgomery
Lydia Miller Middleton
Lyndon Orr
M. H. Adams
Margaret E. Sangster
Margaret Vandercook
Maria Edgeworth
Maria Thompson Daviess
Mariano Azuela
Marion Polk Angellotti
Mark Overton
Mark Twain
Mary Austin
Mary Cole
Mary Rowlandson
Mary Wollstonecraft
Shelley
Max Beerbohm
Myra Kelly
Nathaniel Hawthrone
O. F. Walton
Oscar Wilde
Owen Johnson
P.G.Wodehouse
Paul and Mable Thorn
Paul G. Tomlinson
Paul Severing
Peter B. Kyne
Plato
R. Derby Holmes
R. L. Stevenson
Rabindranath Tagore
Rahul Alvares
Ralph Waldo Emmerson
Rene Descartes
Rex E. Beach
Richard Harding Davis
Richard Jefferies
Robert Barr
Robert Frost
Robert Gordon Anderson
Robert L. Drake
Robert Lansing
Robert Michael Ballantyne
Robert W. Chambers
Rosa Nouchette Carey
Ross Kay
Rudyard Kipling
Samuel B. Allison
Samuel Hopkins Adams
Sarah Bernhardt
Selma Lagerlof
Sherwood Anderson
Sigmund Freud
Standish O'Grady
Stanley Weyman
Stella Benson
Stephen Crane
Stewart Edward White
Stijn Streuvels
Swami Abhedananda
Swami Parmananda
T. S. Ackland
The Princess Der Ling
Thomas A. Janvier
Thomas A Kempis
Thomas Anderton
Thomas Bailey Aldrich
Thomas Bulfinch
Thomas De Quincey
Thomas H. Huxley
Thomas Hardy
Thomas More
Thornton W. Burgess
U. S. Grant
Valentine Williams
Victor Appleton
Virginia Woolf
Walter Scott
Washington Irving
Wilbur Lawton
Wilkie Collins
Willa Cather
Willard F. Baker
William Makepeace
Thackeray
William W. Walter
Winston Churchill
Yei Theodora Ozaki
Young E. Allison
Zane Grey

www.ingramcontent.com/pod-product-compliance
Lightning Source LLC
LaVergne TN
LVHW091640100826
845152LV00006B/113/J

* 9 7 8 1 4 2 1 8 1 4 5 0 6 *